HARD CODE

MISHA BELL

♠ Mozaika Publications ♠

Copyright © 2020 Misha Bell
www.mishabell.com

Published by Mozaika Publications, an imprint of Mozaika LLC.
www.mozaikallc.com

Cover by Najla Qamber Designs
www.najlaqamberdesigns.com

Photography by Wander Aguiar
www.wanderbookclub.com

ISBN: 978-1-63142-621-6
Print ISBN: 978-1-63142-622-3

Chapter One

"You hired a hooker to test a bunch of sex toys?"

"Use your inside voice!" I hiss at Ava, my face burning as I scan the other Starbucks patrons waiting in line with us. Most have headphones plugged into their ears and are lost inside their phones, but still. What if someone overhears?

She grins mischievously and lowers her voice to the closest thing to a whisper she's capable of. "Only if you spill all the gory details."

"Fine. First and foremost, Dominika is *not* a hooker. She's a showgirl."

"Wait." Ava's amber eyes glint impishly. "Is this the 'showgirl' from the strip club Voldemort dragged you to in Prague? The one who violated the nuns on stage?"

"She was playing the role of a succubus. They weren't real nuns."

Her reminder of He Who Must Not Be Named—a.k.a. my ex—only increases my discomfort. I went to that club to prove to Bob that I wasn't a prude, but he broke up with me anyway.

Ava knows me well, which is why she launches into something guaranteed to distract me. Raising her voice an octave, she says, "I'm surprised the Rockettes aren't putting on a show like that for Christmas. One of them could penetrate a faux nun with a strap-on, another with a fist—"

"Hush!" My cheeks are hot enough to make an omelet on them. "I needed someone with experience using sex toys, so I hired her, okay?"

"Uh-huh." Ava steps forward as the line moves. "For your new QA project."

I cast another furtive glance around us. "Like I said, I'm testing an app for a teledildonics company."

"Teledildonics," she repeats, savoring the word. "The prefix *tele* refers to long distance; the suffix *onics* means pertaining to, and the root is *dildo*... as in the thing I've been convincing you to try." Her voice grows louder. "Are we talking about long-distance dildos?"

As I cringe, I make a mental vow: I will get her back for this. She will rue this day.

"Precisely." I'm proud of how even my voice is. "The app I'll be testing lets one user control a device being utilized by another user over the internet."

"Sure. Sure." She makes her face look serious. "To put that in layman's terms: a dildo will go into

Dominika in Prague, and you will make her come with the app from New York."

At this point, it's not just my treacherous cheeks that are red—my ears are too. "It's called end-to-end testing. It needs to be as close to the way the product is going to be used in the real world as possible."

"Or rear-end testing." She waggles her eyebrows suggestively. When I pointedly turn my back to her, she laughs and says, "Isn't that basically having sex with Dominika? After paying her? How is she not a hooker then?"

The reality is actually worse. Dominika and *her boyfriend* will be participating in the testing, but I'm not telling Ava this now. Or maybe ever. "Fine. She's not just a showgirl. Happy now?"

"Hey." She finally lowers her voice. "I have nothing against the world's oldest profession. If I hadn't already wasted years on medical school, and if all the johns were hot and STDs didn't exist, I'd sign up. At least if it paid well and I wasn't dating anyone. Especially if I was as orgasm-deprived as you. Come to think of it—"

Thankfully, it's our turn to order now. She gets enough caffeine to send a rhino bouncing off the walls, and I request my venti chamomile tea in the hopes of calming down before the meeting I've been dreading.

We step aside to wait for our drinks, and Ava grins like the Grinch. "So, back to teledildonics."

Before I can shush her again, *he* comes in.

I forget what I was about to say. I forget to *breathe*.

Carved features that remind me equally of Greek gods and angels, eyes the deep blue hue of a lapis lazuli stone, framed by stylish horn-rimmed glasses. Lips that beg to be kissed. Shaggy jet-black hair, with a stray strand that falls in the middle of his face and just begs me to walk over and brush it back—which I'd have to reach high to do because he's at least a foot taller than me. Despite the warm weather, he's dressed in a black trench coat with a black shirt underneath, an outfit that accentuates the powerful breadth of his shoulders and—

"Earth to Fanny." Ava's voice intrudes into my oxytocin-addled brain.

I spin around before she realizes I was checking out Hottie McDark. Knowing her, she'd push me at him, or nag me into starting a conversation, or do a million other things that would embarrass me straight into a panic attack.

Someone like me and a guy that hot do not mix.

Before she can resume pestering me about teledildonics within possible earshot of Hottie McDark, I preemptively jam my hand into my pocket and pull out one of my most treasured possessions—my phone, a.k.a. Precious. "You have to see the app I created," I tell Ava and steal a glance behind me.

Did Hottie McDark's eyebrows lift at the mention of an app?

Nah. Nor, despite appearances, is he looking at

me right now. He's probably studying the menu board directly behind me.

"Okay…" Ava sounds as enthusiastic as I do when she shares a horribly gross story about her residency in the ER. "It lets you cartoon yourself, right?"

"Nope." I bring up the app and stare proudly at the crisp user interface that I toiled over for months. "It tells you which cartoon character you most resemble."

"Potato potahto. But I'll bite. Who do *I* look like?"

Feeling a little naughty, I position her just right and snap an image with the app. Except I aim the camera at Hottie McDark instead of Ava—and the app promptly brings up a cartoon character: Clark Kent from *Superman,* the animated series.

I can see that. That strand of hair, the glasses, and the chiseled features do match. The evil genius of this move is that the app also stores the original photo, so I could, should I wish, backward search from the image to, say, his social media profile.

Assuming I wanted to become a stalker, that is.

Before Ava catches on, I aim the camera at her and snap another pic.

"You're Belle." I show her the doe-eyed, brown-haired image on the phone. "From *Beauty and the Beast.*"

"Tale as old as time," she singsongs. "I guess that's a compliment. Can I do you?"

"Be our guest." I thrust the phone into her hands,

mostly because I want to see if she can figure out how to use the app without my help.

To my great relief, she figures it out on the fly. This isn't as good as a grandmother test, but close. I had to teach Ava how to program her universal remote control.

When the app gives her the result, she chuckles. "Snow White. Is it always a Disney Princess?"

"Not always."

"I bet it's your easy-to-blush pale cheeks." She examines me closely. "Or the round face."

I sneak another peek at Hottie McDark. "I'm just glad it's not one of the seven dwarves."

"Oh yeah, put a beard on you, and you'd be a dead ringer for Bashful."

I cringe. Her voice is the loudest it's been yet; the guy would have to be deaf not to notice us at this point. "Please keep it down."

"Sorry." She hands me my phone back. "Are you going to make any money on this app?"

I glance at the time to make sure I'm not running late before I pocket Precious. "The app is free. I even made it opensource, so anyone can take and use my code however they wish."

"Is it for that promotion you want, then?"

I shrug. "Not a promotion, a lateral move. The app was to prove to myself that I have what it takes to be a developer. Now I just need to make the people at work believe in me too, or at least value me enough to give me a chance to switch departments."

In the corner of my eye, I see Hottie McDark placing his order, which means if we don't get our drinks soon, he'll be standing close enough for me to smell him.

Or touch.

Or—

"And this smart sex toys project will help?" Ava asks, again speaking too loudly for my comfort.

"Our company owner himself wrote the app. That makes the testing as high profile as it gets." I strain to hear what the guy is ordering but only make out the word *tea*—and it's nice to know there's another sucker out there willing to pay a huge premium for a bag of dried leaves.

"And said owner is the infamous Vlad the Impaler, right?" She says the name with relish.

"That's what the rumor mill at the office calls him. I'm sure he's Mr. Vladimir Chortsky to his face."

"Or Master," she says in her best Renfield voice. "And you're meeting him today? Shouldn't there be garlic around your neck, or a cross inside your panties?"

I chuckle nervously. "They do say he never sleeps. Or at least he answers emails at any time, day or night."

Ava makes a swoony face. "Does he glitter?"

"I'll find out today." Hottie McDark is now walking our way, so it takes everything I have to keep my cool. "I checked out his code for this app, and it was very elegant and inventive—appropriate for a centuries-old creature of the night. My boss, Sandra, also told me that when he writes something, he doesn't work with the development team, yet the resulting apps never have any bugs—"

"How not thrilling." Ava exaggeratedly yawns. "What I want to know is: Has he impaled any female employees?"

Sensual notes of tangerine and bergamot waft into my nostrils.

Someone's tea or Hottie McDark's cologne? He's now right next to me, so close that I don't dare look at him lest I melt into a puddle. My heart hammers unevenly, and I can feel a new wave of hot color washing into my cheeks.

"Fanny. Ava." The barista slams our drinks on the counter.

Perfect. Before Ava can further embarrass me in front of Hottie McDark, I snatch my drink, thrust hers into her hand, and drag her out of the Starbucks by her elbow.

"I have to go to work," I say when we get outside. Right away, the deafening honking of taxis fills my ears. We're across the street from Battery Park, with the Statue of Liberty visible in the distance.

Ava pecks me on the cheek. "Good luck. And if the Impaler turns you into a vampire, you must do the same to me as soon as you can. I can steal us blood bags from the hospital."

I sneak a final longing glance at Hottie McDark through the tinted glass. "You better be on your best behavior, or I'll just make you my blood whore instead."

She laughs as she walks away, and I sprint to the nearby skyscraper and ride the elevator to my company's floor.

Exiting, I survey my surroundings. *Binary Birch*, the plaque on the wall states in a very serious-looking font. The cold utilitarian nature of the modern décor hasn't changed since I was here for my in-person interviews a few months back. No game rooms or sleeping nooks like they might have at other, hipper software companies—not with the Impaler at the helm.

The people around me are mostly strangers. The company policy is that everyone has the option of working remotely if they wish, so I've been working from home and communicating with the office via email, instant messenger, and occasionally, a teleconferencing app.

I pull out Precious and check the time. Ten minutes until I have to brave the Impaler's office.

Sipping my tea, I jump on the Wi-Fi and check my messages.

Sandra, the QA manager and my direct boss, wants to see me if I have the time.

I head into the maze of cubicles. Since she's one of the few people I know by sight, I locate her quickly and knock on the glass wall of her cube.

"Hi, Sandra," I say when she tears her gaze from her screen.

"Oh, hey, Fanny. There you are." With a prim smile, she stands up and leads us to a small meeting room.

"So," she says, not meeting my gaze as we sit down across from each other. "I just wanted to double check… You're okay with the eccentric testing project you're about to undertake, right?"

"I am," I state as confidently as I can fake it.

I know why she keeps asking. The last thing the company wants is for me to file a sexual harassment suit over this, or for me to say that I'm not cool with it when I speak to the Impaler, thus making her, my manager, look like an idiot.

"I'm glad," she says, and we quickly go over the project I've just finished testing, an app that works with a wristband fitness tracker.

She smiles when I tell her that I even lost a few pounds thanks to all the walking to test the pedometer functionality.

Then it's time for the meeting I've been dreading, and Sandra leads me to the only non-glass-walled office on the floor.

According to some jokes, the Impaler doesn't like the light, and according to others, he needs the privacy to make his kills in peace.

"Want me to take that?" Sandra asks, worriedly eyeing my almost empty cup.

"No drinks allowed in there?" I ask.

She darts a nervous glance at the door. "I better take it."

As I hand her the cup, my previously steady hand begins to tremble.

How scary can our glorious leader be?

"Keep me in the loop." Sandra opens the door for me.

Feeling like a lamb going to the proverbial slaughter, I shuffle into the Impaler's lair—and before I can catch sight of the man himself, my manager helpfully closes the door behind me, like a vampire's minion springing a trap.

Soft music is vibrating the airwaves in here. *In the Hall of the Mountain King* by Edvard Grieg—a fitting melody to get exsanguinated to.

I catch a whiff of tangerine and bergamot, and my stomach drops.

Can't be.

I turn around.

Illuminated by the bluish light of a large monitor is the gorgeous face of the stranger I was just drooling over at Starbucks.

Even his tea is here, on his spotlessly clean desk.

"Hello, Ms. Pack," Vlad the Impaler says with a slight Transylvanian accent. "Good to finally meet you."

Chapter Two

*T*he accent is actually Russian—everyone knows that much about our reclusive CEO. And his place of birth might be why he addressed me so formally; I've read that in Russia, they often use the plural *you* and patronymics, both as a sign of respect and to separate close friends from strangers.

Ms. Pack is a decent English equivalent, except that it makes me sound like Ms. Pac-Man: round and starving for doughnut holes. And sidebar—shouldn't that game have been called Pac-Woman, or Ms. Pac? Actually, thank god it wasn't Ms. Pac; that's too close to home and I was teased enough being Fanny Pack as it is.

Then blood leaves my face.

He could've overheard me and Ava. What was the last—

I realize he's suddenly looming over me, hand outstretched, like Nosferatu.

Must've used his preternatural vampire speed to leap out from behind his desk and dash toward me before my brain could process it.

Crap. How long have I been standing here, ignoring that hand? And how the hell did this happen? How is Vlad the Impaler Hottie McDark? All the rumors about this man skipped a critical detail: how mouthwateringly attractive he is.

"Are you okay?" the Impaler asks, his accent thickening.

Ugh, now I'm ogling him. And still ignoring that hand. Gathering my courage, I stick out my arm and clasp his much, much bigger palm.

Holy estrogen.

My heart rate spikes, and a jolt of orgasmic energy spreads through my body, electrocuting a nest of angry butterflies in my stomach before settling somewhere low in my core.

How many hours is it socially appropriate to hold a hand like this?

Reluctantly, I peel my fingers away from his.

He looks down at me, his expression completely unreadable. He's either an amazing poker player or this handshake didn't affect him at all.

"Take a seat." He gestures at the chair in front of his desk, and by the time I plop into it, he's already in his. It's Embody by Herman Miller, the very chair I have at home, only mine is blue while his is black.

He lowers the music volume with a small remote.

"You have a great reputation at Binary Birch, Ms. Pack."

I do? That's news. Even if that were true, how would he know that?

I don't dare ask as that might be as suicidal as reciprocating by telling him his reputation *isn't* so stellar.

"Thank you," I stammer before the silence veers into uncomfortable territory. "I love working here." And by *love*, I mean *tolerate*. But what's a little white lie between a monster and his prey?

He stares at me, and I feel like I might drown in the lapis depths of his eyes. "The project I'm trusting you with is extremely important."

I bob my head up and down so vigorously, I nearly give myself whiplash.

"The client—Belka—will get a chance to demonstrate the final product to the editors of *Cosmopolitan* magazine in two weeks." He peers at me as though to verify that I know what *Cosmo* is, so I blush and nod, just in case. "That is a huge opportunity." His dark eyebrows furrow minutely as he finishes with, "We can't let Belka down."

"Yes, sir." I give him a crisp military salute.

Wait, what? Why did I do that?

There's no hint of amusement on his face. He must be used to such gestures from back when he participated in Napoleonic wars and what-not.

He steeples his fingers. "I realize you must have the most thorough testing plan in mind."

Actually, I have the desire to suck on those long, masculine fingers in mind at the moment, but I keep that to myself.

"I hope you will let me enrich your plan with some extra test cases—which may already overlap with yours." He reaches into his desk and takes out a couple of stapled sheets of paper.

Only now do I realize that he's basically telling me how to do my job—which would be like me teaching him how to properly drink blood. Control freak much?

As I snatch the papers, our fingers brush for a second, sending another dozen joules of electricity into my lower regions.

Flushing, I glance at what I'm holding.

Hmm. Pink paper. A faint smell of perfume. Pretty cursive with hearts dotting the occasional "i." A woman must've put this together for him, and not Sandra, whose scent is more evocative of boiled cabbage. Besides, Sandra is obsessed with electronic communication, judging by all the constant "Save a Tree" propaganda in her email signature.

The pang of jealously I suddenly experience is as inappropriate as it is insane.

To avoid dwelling on it, I skim the content of the paper—and as I do, I feel the flush spread to my ears and chest, turning them beet red.

There are items like "was orgasm achieved?" and "how many times?"

I have the former in my testing plan already, but

not the latter—which, of course, isn't the source of my discombobulation.

It's just that reading the word *orgasm* in his presence feels wrong.

And dirty.

And somehow hot all at the same time.

I better get out of here with what passes for my remaining dignity.

"I will make sure to, um… utilize this"—I fan myself with the papers—"in my testing."

He reaches under the desk, yanks something out, and places it on the desk between us.

I gape at it.

Strictly speaking, it's a carry-on suitcase—but only in the same sense as a disco ball is a globe. It's covered in frilly polka dots and bejeweled with so many differently colored stones, you'd think a rainbow-farting unicorn had ejaculated on it.

As I look closer, I realize most of the designs are not polka dots but tiny multicolored penises and vaginas that someone painstakingly drew by hand.

At least I hope it was by hand.

My cheeks veer off the red end of the visible spectrum, radiating as much infrared as a welding torch.

Annoyingly, Vlad's face only shows the neutral professionalism he's been displaying throughout this whole encounter. Maybe he's one of Anne Rice's vampires—her older ones become as if made of stone over time.

"The hardware is inside," he says.

A hybrid between a hiccup and a giggle escapes my throat.

He just called a collection of dildos *hardware,* and probably not as a joke.

"Got it." I leap to my feet and reach for the suitcase just as he slides it forward.

Our fingers brush, generating enough of that electric jolt to power the toys for a week. I swallow and yank the suitcase off the desk.

It's heavy. There must be more than a few dildos, and who knows what else.

I hope Dominika's vagina can handle it all. Not to mention, shipping this "hardware" to the Czech Republic will cost a small fortune. I really hope no one at the DHL office asks me what's inside. For that matter, I pray no one here at the office asks me "What's with the suitcase?" as I sprint to the elevator.

"It was good to meet you," I tell Vlad and prepare to make the sprint.

"Will I see you at the monthly meeting in five minutes?" he asks.

I nearly drop my genital-inscribed luggage.

In theory, everyone is supposed to attend the monthly meeting. Its purpose is for us to have an idea of what the rest of Binary Birch is working on, find opportunities for synergy, and other corporate speak gobbledygook. In practice, since I've been working from home, I typically dial into this meeting on the phone, then promptly tune most of it out as I do my actual job of testing.

I do know one thing: the Impaler is famous for never joining this meeting in person either—and he doesn't have the work-from-home excuse. He just dials in and never says a word, though people claim to get emails about some things discussed at the meeting, hinting that he actually listens—which is why everyone is always on their best behavior during it.

Yet he said "see you," not "hear you," so tradition is about to be broken for some reason.

Of course, now I have to attend the meeting.

With this suitcase.

Shoot me now.

"Affirmative," I reply belatedly and fight another urge to salute. "See you soon."

Gracelessly, I spin around and head for the door, eager to escape the lair and its vampiric occupant.

His voice stops me as I'm reaching for the door handle. "By the way, Ms. Pack…" he says to my back, and for the first time, I detect a hint of emotion in his tone. "You should know something. I don't impale my employees."

Chapter Three

Suitcase in hand, I shoot out of the Impaler's office to the bathroom as if the hounds of hell were on my heels. A single thought spins through my mind like a broken vinyl record.

He heard us at Starbucks.

At least the part about him impaling female employees.

What else did he hear?

How screwed am I?

"What the bejesus is that?" asks an attractive black-haired woman as I come out of my stall.

I dart an awkward glance at the suitcase I left by one of the sinks. "My niece's school bag."

I don't have a niece, but if I did, and this *were* her school bag, she'd need serious therapy.

The stranger looks at me like I'm some exotic cricket in a terrarium. "I'm Britney Archibald."

This day is getting worse and worse. Though I've

never seen her in person or on video, we know each other—at least over instant messenger and email.

She's one of the five women working in the development department, and I recently tested some code she wrote.

Unfortunately, unlike the rest of her department, she's not a very good programmer—or at least, she's a careless one—because I found a plethora of bugs in her app, much more than usual. She turned out to have a paper-thin skin when it came to my findings, and her correspondence with me took an adversarial turn. I've tried to patch things up, especially since I'm angling to be in her department, but she's rebuffed my attempts to jump on a video call and clear the air.

The only reason I haven't escalated this to our managers is that I'm not a snitch. Plus, rumor has it that Britney is a much better hacker than she is a developer. Apparently, after she broke up with one guy in the sales department, she hacked into his social media accounts and made his profile images a photo of him during some sort of pony play.

Just my luck to bump into her, of all people, with the genitalia-decorated atrocity in my possession.

I call forth all of my professionalism and extend my hand. "I'm Fanny Pack."

She glares at my palm in disgust.

Oh, shit. I haven't washed my hands yet—and I doubt she'll accept "urine is sterile" as an excuse.

I also see her eyes narrow as she recalls why my name is familiar.

"Good to put a face to a name," I blurt, and grabbing the suitcase, I sprint for the door. Over my shoulder, I add, "See you at the monthly meeting."

I think she replies with something catty, but I don't catch what it is.

I rush to the pantry and wash my hands in the sink there. Then I down a glass of water and sneak into the large conference room where the monthly meeting is going to take place.

Great.

I'm the first one here.

I take the chair in the farthest corner and stash the suitcase under the table.

There. No one should see it now, and the comfort of my knees is a small price to pay.

As I wait for the rest of the employees to file in, I get Precious off the company's Wi-Fi and search the internet for information about the Impaler.

It's eerie how little I find.

He's obscenely rich—but I already knew that. He owns a successful software company—I work there, so duh.

There are no pictures of him online. Not on the Binary Birch website, nor in the newspapers, nor anywhere else I look. If I hadn't snapped his pic with my app, I would've been sure he's the type of vampire that doesn't reflect in mirrors or appear in photos.

He also doesn't have a social media profile of any kind, not even a professional one, like LinkedIn. My

Starbucks idea to backward search him via that photo would've failed.

Of course, I don't need to do that now. I know who he is, and any sort of romance is out of the question. He's my boss's boss—or boss squared—not to mention a notorious workaholic who doesn't have time for anything else in his life.

Besides, I'm sure he wouldn't be interested in someone who works for him—as that would involve impaling that someone, and he said he doesn't do that to employees. And even if impaling were on the table, I'm sure he wouldn't want to do it to me.

I shouldn't even be thinking in this direction, not at such a pivotal moment in my career.

And yet, I create a Google alert for his name. This way, if something about him does show up online, I'll be the first to know.

A door slams, making my head jerk up.

As I stash Precious in my pocket, I realize the room is now packed—and the man I was just cyberstalking is standing at the head of the table, his rich blue eyes gleaming intensely behind his glasses.

I gulp.

Usually, one of the project managers chairs this meeting, but right now, their whole team is cowering in the corner.

At least the men. The women in this room appear to be spontaneously ovulating.

Britney is practically choking on her drool, and

even Sandra—who must be at least thirty years his senior—is nearly as red as I am.

"For the last few months, I've been working on Project Belka," the Impaler says without so much as a "howdy y'all." "It's now in the testing stage." He glances at me for a heartbeat, and Britney's eyes turn my way, then narrow into slits.

I sink lower in my seat and do my best tortoise impersonation. For the love of C++, please don't tell them about the suitcase full of sex toys. Pretty please, with a gallon of the juiciest blood on top.

He doesn't.

Instead, he moves his gaze to where the accountants are sitting. "If the QA team files any expense reports tagged *Belka*, the paperwork is to be expedited. If you have *any* questions about the whys of the reports, direct those to me."

The expressions on the faces of the accounting team imply there will be no questions. Ever.

This is actually great. I really wanted to expense the exuberant shipping costs I'm about to accrue, but without his executive order, I wouldn't have bothered. The accounting team gave me a runaround when I ordered myself an ergonomic keyboard, and that's as work-related as any expense can get.

But how did he know? Is he a precognitive vampire, a la Alice in *Twilight*?

"This goes for everything else." His gaze sweeps the room, lingering on me for a second. "Project Belka is a priority."

Wow.

No pressure or anything.

Did Sandra just sneak a guilty glance at me? She *was* the one who assigned me to this project, but then again, given how important this thing is turning out to be, she'd kind of paid me the compliment of "let's throw the most likely to survive under that bus."

Britney raises her hand with the excitement of a grade-schooler who knows the answer to something for the first time in her life.

Ignoring her, the Impaler turns on his heel and strides out of the room.

"Do you need any help?" Britney shouts at his back. "I can code review if—"

The door slams behind him.

The room takes a collective relieved breath— everyone except Britney, that is. She looks like someone has just shaved her beloved pet tarantula.

The conference bridge phone beeps, notifying us that the Impaler has just rejoined the meeting as his usual ghostly presence.

One of the project managers takes over the meeting, but I can't follow what he or anyone says due to all the adrenaline coursing through my system.

This project is mega important.

I can't mess it up.

To soothe myself, I take out Precious.

Pretending like I'm glancing at an important memo, I bring up my app and use it on my coworkers.

Sandra's cartoon doppelgänger turns out to be

Dory from *Finding Nemo*. Britney gets Maleficent—no surprise there. Someone in sales reminds the app of Sylvester J. Pussycat, a woman in accounting is Pepe Le Pew, while two guys from the development department match Beavis and Butt-Head.

Seeing most of my fellow employees like this makes me realize something: The ratio of women to men in the development department, and the company overall, is much higher than for the software industry at large. This is especially interesting in light of said ratio in the educational system. When I was taking computer science courses at Brooklyn College, I was often the only female in my class.

Is the Impaler behind this, or the HR department? If it's the Impaler, color me impressed—with his vampiric lifespan, he might've grown up when the glass ceiling was two inches above the floor.

Well, whoever's behind it, it's one less thing to worry about when it comes to moving to the dev department.

Speaking of which, I feel more determined to do that now than ever. In fact, I think I should make my request ASAP. At first, I was waiting for the completion of the Belka project, but thanks to this meeting, I've earned some visibility and there probably won't be a better time.

For the rest of the meeting, I play out different versions of my "move" pitch in my mind.

When it's over, I wait for everyone to leave before I deal with the suitcase again.

Sylvester J. Pussycat and Pepe Le Pew are among the last to leave, with Beavis and Butt-Head on their tails.

Only Sandra is left now, and she's clearly stayed back on purpose.

Whatever her reason, I decide to seize the moment before I chicken out. "Hi, Sandra. There's something important I wanted to talk to you about."

She pales. I bet she thinks I'm about to flake on the testing project.

Before she can have a heart attack, I hit her with my real agenda, and as she listens, some color returns to her cheeks.

"Do you have any experience coding?" she asks when I'm done making my case. "This is the first thing they'll ask me when I bring this up."

I tell her about my app and offer to share a link to the source control database, so she can pass it on to whoever wants to see what I'm capable of.

"Please," she says. "I'll get that over to everyone on the development team, along with a glowing recommendation from me."

I beam at her. "I'm sorry to leave your team. Testing isn't—"

She waves this off. "It will be a shame to lose you, but you have to think about your career first and foremost." She darts a furtive glance at the door and unplugs the conference room phone. "I wanted to talk to you about something as well. I know you always do a great job, but please do your best when it comes to the Belka project. I'm worried that if something were to go wrong, both our jobs would be on the line."

Great.

I'll either get the position I want, or lose my job altogether.

"I got it," I say with a confidence I wish I felt. "Leave it to me."

Sandra plugs the phone back in. "Let me know if there's anything I can do to help."

"I'll do that." I smile and hope she'll leave.

She stands there.

"Bye," I say.

She frowns. "You're not leaving yet?"

"Have to check on an email," I lie.

Though she's in the loop on the sex toy testing, I still don't want her to see the suitcase.

"Good luck," she says and finally leaves.

I wait another minute for everyone to disperse to their cubicles, then snatch the sex toy carry-on from under the table and sprint out of the meeting room— and nearly tackle Britney, who's lurking in the corridor on the way to the elevators.

"Fanny." Her voice is laced with poisoned honey. "I'm glad I bumped into you."

She is? Is hell experiencing climate change?

"I wanted to ask you about the Belka project," she says.

Ah. There it is.

"Please direct all your inquiries to Mr. Chortsky," I say politely.

I can see she's unhappy with that answer, so I clutch the suitcase and step forward, hoping to quickly get past her.

She doesn't move.

"Excuse me," I mutter. "I'm late for a meeting." With that, I forcefully squeeze myself between her and the wall and rush into the elevator as if I were being chased by an evil fairy.

Once outside the building, I speed-walk all the way to the DHL office on Church Street.

Wiping the sweat from my brow—it really is warm outside—I scan the paperwork involved.

This day gets better and better. The customs form has an item list on it.

This should be fun.

I locate the nearest bathroom, lock myself in a stall, and open the suitcase.

Fuck me. This is a lot of toys.

A dildo in a clear plastic box. Something that looks like a buttplug. A cock ring. A vibrator. And lots of items I don't even recognize.

Luckily, there is a type of menu here, written by the same female hand as the auxiliary testing cases sheet. In fact, the inside of the suitcase also smells like that same perfume.

I wonder if she's the Impaler's lover. That might explain why he's giving this such a high priority.

Kill her, the green monster of jealousy shouts inside my head.

I don't know who she is, I reply. *You've got to chill.*

Find out and rip her hair out.

You're nuts.

I'm you.

Silencing the green monster, I pocket the list, close the suitcase, and get back into the main DHL office.

Has anyone blushed this much filling out a customs form before? My face is so hot I worry my hair will catch on fire.

When the form is done, I get into the line and wait.

And wait.

Growing bored, I take out my phone.

Hmm. An email from Dominika.

When I read the subject, my heart rate speeds up.

I'm sorry.

No.

Can't be.

I open the email, scan it, and nearly drop Precious.

It's my worst nightmare come true.

Dominika won't be my tester.

Chapter Four

The car ride home happens in a confused haze.

Dominika's email almost seems like a cruel joke.

Apparently, she's joining a convent tomorrow. She, the woman who pretended to seduce—and then creatively violate—all the orifices of "nuns" at a strip club.

I fire off an email asking her if she's kidding, only to get an instant autoreply reiterating her plans to become a nun.

If I tell Ava, she'll die of laughter at my expense. Dominika the Nun will have a forked tongue and will be covered from head to toe in tattoos, some of which depict sexual acts prohibited by the sacred texts.

Entering my apartment, I feed Monkey, my guinea pig. Originally, she was a gift to my ex, but he didn't want her, so I ended up with her in the reverse of a custody battle.

"What do I do now?" I ask her when she's done with her chow.

The little rodent hops up and down as though she's dancing.

"You're no help," I say, then refresh her water and pace the apartment as I ponder my situation.

I thought I'd gotten a lucky break with Dominika. She's an expert with toys, lives impressively far away, and was willing. I guess the far away part isn't a big deal—I can use a proxy server to simulate that with someone local if I want. But the willingness to shove toys into holes is harder to find.

I meet Monkey's pink eyes. "Do you think I should hire a prostitute?"

She scurries into the little house she usually sleeps in.

Judgmental much?

I resume my pacing and think further about prostitution.

The biggest problem is that it's illegal in New York. More importantly, I have no clue where to find one. Or a pimp. Do they still use pimps?

Either way, I doubt you can just place an ad for a hooker on a freelancer site.

Damn Giuliani—or whoever it was that cleaned up 42nd Street. Back in the day, you could hire a sex worker *there.*

Maybe I could put an ad on Craigslist?

A quick search later, I learn that they got rid of the relevant section of the site, and some other similar services, like Backpage, got shut down completely.

As I read up on the topic, I realize that by hiring a sex worker, I could inadvertently end up supporting the evil that is human trafficking.

So that's a no-go.

Would women working in a local strip club be interested in this? Or some escort service, perhaps?

Are traffickers involved with *that*?

Unlikely, but not sure I want to risk it. With hindsight, even Dominika could've been a victim of exploitation. Maybe it's for the best that she backed out.

So where does that leave me?

A silly idea crosses my mind.

Sandra said to let her know if there's anything she can do to help.

I picture myself approaching my boss for this and preemptively die of mortified laughter. Apart from the obvious, what if she has a weak heart and dies on me? I'd be infamous as the weirdest murderer in the history of crime.

But asking a woman I know *is* a promising direction.

Would Ava help?

She swears by her vibrator.

Obviously, she'd never let me live this down, but at least I'd keep my job.

The phone rings.

Speak of the devil.

"Hi, Ava," I say, snatching up Precious. "Are you having a slow day at the hospital?"

"How did your meeting go?" she asks. "Any impaling I should be aware of?"

I tell her everything but tone down my reactions to my boss's boss because… well, because.

Sure enough, she's choking on laughter when I get to the part where I lost my sex toy tester to a convent.

"So," I say at the end, "there's a pretty big favor I want to ask you."

"Noooo," she squeezes out in between hysterical giggles. "I'm not having cybersex with you."

"That wasn't the favor," I lie. "I was wondering if—"

"Dude," Ava says. "You don't have a problem."

"I don't?"

"You should test it on yourself," she says with a giggle. "It'll be fun, and you haven't had an orgasm since what's-his-name before Bob."

"But—"

"Wouldn't it be nice to loosen up a little?"

I squeeze Precious tighter, the mention of my ex and the phrase "loosen up" tempting me to say something very unkind to my bestie.

The reason He Who Shouldn't Have Been Named broke up with me was that I wasn't "adventurous enough, sexually."

Those words sting to this very day, especially because there might've been a kernel of truth in them. Not that Bob was any kind of wizard in bed… not even a Hufflepuff.

Ava's tone turns serious. "I didn't mean that, I'm sorry. I just stuck my big foot in my mouth."

"More like your whole butt." The grumpiness in my voice is only partially faked.

"Look," she says with a sigh. "If you really insist, I'll think about being your tester."

"No, it's okay." I pinch the bridge of my nose. "You might have a point. I shouldn't ask you to do something I'm not willing to do myself. The problem is, even if I do it, I still need a guy for the male toys."

She snorts. "I wouldn't worry about that. Crook your finger at the first male you see, preferably of legal age, and he'll test whatever you want."

"Uh-huh. It might work like that for *you*."

"It would work like that for pretty much anyone with a uterus. But let's say it doesn't. You can still get on Tinder or something like that. Tell the guys who match with you that you want cybersex before your dates and see how enthused they'll get."

That actually does sound more plausible, though when I try to picture it, I feel deeply uneasy. Also, for some reason, the only image that forms in my mind is of lapis lazuli eyes and—

"Ooh, sorry," Ava says. "They're paging me."

"Wait, I—"

The phone goes dead.

Paging. Still. Leave it to the medical profession to

live in the Stone Age. I wonder if they also have dialup modems at the hospital, or cassette tapes.

Hey, at least they no longer use leeches, so that's progress.

Unless they still do?

A quick search on Precious later, I learn that they do indeed still utilize the little blood-sucking monsters, and that the FDA somehow managed to classify leeches as a "living medical device to clear localized blood clots."

The article mentions that maggots are used too, and I stop reading there, because gross.

Monkey peeks out of her cage and squeaks.

I give her half of a grape. "I know, I'm procrastinating."

Snatching the grape, Monkey hides in her little house.

Fine. I can figure this out on my own.

Jumping on my laptop, I open a fresh spreadsheet, name it "testing on myself," and fill out two columns: pro and con.

Under "con" are things like: "might be hard to face my coworkers afterward, especially the Impaler" and "it's a less realistic test than if there were a second person involved."

In the "pro" column are tidbits such as: "keep my job," "Ava might be right and this could be fun," and "prove ex wrong."

Since the pro column ends up longer, I reluctantly accept the inevitable.

"I'll be my own guinea pig," I say out loud. "No offense, Monkey."

Precious pings.

It's a text from Ava.

So? You doing it?

I reply with the okay sign.

I'd wax if I were you. Makes one feel sexy.

Seriously? I text back.

Like a heart attack. Now stop beating around the bush and get rid of your bush. Emojis of lips, cat face, cherries, flower, peace sign, wishbone, hot spot, and peach are followed by a razor.

I didn't even know there was a razor emoji.

Silencing the phone, I dart a glance at the suitcase.

Nope.

Not ready yet.

Maybe Ava is right. Would I be more eager if I made myself prettier down under?

Since the jungle that is my legs is on my to-do list anyway, I'll just do that and some ladyscaping at the same time. The breakup with my ex made me experiment a little in this area. I've tried styling my pubes geometrically with upside-down and regular triangles, aeronautically with a landing strip, and—briefly—what could best be described as a dictator's mustache.

Speaking of, what's with all the dictators sporting a 'stache? I bet one started the trend, and the dictator-sheep copycatted. Come to think of it, their inspiration might've been the original Vlad the Impaler. The painting of him had a mustache so big and bushy, he probably had a pet name for it, like Pufos—which means fluffy in Romanian.

Thank the hipster gods "my" Impaler doesn't have such a crime against nature above his kissable lips. He only has a little bit of sexy stubble up there—just the way I like it.

In any case, nowadays I'm sporting a retro bush of epic proportions, with cobwebs and tumbleweeds down there, and "No Trespassing" signs. This isn't a feminist statement, unfortunately, just a sign of self-neglect.

Well, even if feeling sexy weren't a goal, getting that hair under control could make locating my bits a little easier for the testing—so off it shall go.

I dart into the closet where I keep my disposable gloves and N95 mask, then take it all to the bathroom, fully aware of how much I look like I'm planning a naughty game of doctor.

There's a fly in my bathroom.

Gross.

I try to evict him, but the clever beastie sneers at my futile attempts, buzzing around tauntingly.

"Fine," I tell him. "This place is about to smell like hair removal cream. If you get wing cancer, don't come crying to me."

Of course, I didn't get the cream to ward off insects. I just happen to hate the stubbly feel of my legs after shaving, and I've never felt masochistic enough to wax.

Stripping down to the buff, I trim the affected area as much as is possible without garden shears. Next, I prepare a wet washcloth by the tub and put on the mask to avoid fumes.

As soon as I strap on the gloves and squeeze out a handful of cream, I feel an itch on the top of my head.

Then my nose itches under the mask.

Then my eye.

Ignoring it all, I get into the tub and slather the cream on my legs.

I glance at my pubes.

Am I really doing this?

I guess I am. I get more cream and go to town in the vaginal region. That done, I awkwardly place one foot on the edge of the tub and upgrade the experience to a full Brazilian—I saw a butt plug in that suitcase, so this might help.

I then wait for the cream to break down my hair's protein structure. Bored, I wonder how the Seven Dwarves would've reacted if they'd walked in on Snow White doing something like this.

Especially Bashful.

The fly lands on my mask.

"Shoo." I swat at him.

He buzzes angrily and scurries over to my forehead.

"Get out!" I swat at him once more. "Perv."

The fly's buzzing sounds indignant as he zooms through the room and slams into the closed window.

Serves him right.

In the next moment, I forget all about the fly because my most private area begins to burn.

Ouch. It's *really* burning—like an STD they punish rapists with in the seventh circle of hell.

I shoot a glance at the clock. It's not the full five minutes yet, plus my legs are fine.

This must be because I switched brands, and some ingredient in this formulation doesn't agree with my bikini area. Which is ironic, given that this brand markets itself as being "for sensitive skin." In defense of the manufacturer, most such creams warn you about using this stuff in the exact area that currently burns. It's just never been a problem for me before, else I would have done a patch test on a small part of my privates instead of going all in.

Grabbing the warm cloth, I rub myself hard enough to start a fire.

There.

No more cream on my vag.

Now my butt burns, so I take care of that next.

Which is when my legs start to itch.

With a growl, I wipe all the melted-looking hair from my legs and wash myself all over with a thoroughness an OCD sufferer would be proud of.

Soon, no sign of the cream remains.

I look down.

Things are angrily red, like I'm some animal in heat.

There goes feeling sexy.

Also, there's a strange sensation on the side of my forehead.

More specifically, the right eyebrow region.

A *burning* sensation.

No. Can't be.

Toweling off in a rush, I leap for the mirror.

Crap! There's a glob of hair removal cream on my right eyebrow.

Did I scratch an itch there without realizing? Or did the cream splatter when I battled the fly?

Either way, I frantically wipe the cream off—and most of my eyebrow goes with it.

I wash my face thoroughly and make sure there's no cream lurking somewhere else—like my scalp or my eyelashes.

Nope. Just lost the pubes, leg hair, and an eyebrow.

In the mirror, my remaining eyebrow makes my expression seem equal parts curious, suspicious, and skeptical despite the fact that I'm feeling none of those things, just shame.

Getting my makeup kit, I try drawing the eyebrow back.

The result is acceptable enough for a teleconference, but if I want to see people face to face, I might have to sacrifice the other eyebrow and draw both.

I'm too traumatized to test anything now, so I spend the rest of the day integrating the handwritten test cases into my electronic list, then expanding the document to accommodate all the diverse contents of the suitcase. I also make sure the resulting document will automatically back up to the cloud. The last thing I want is to go through the testing, only to lose the documentation thanks to a busted hard drive and have to start over again.

It's happened to me once, and it was the worst feeling imaginable.

By the time I head to bed, the redness from the hair removal debacle has subsided, and as my head hits the pillow, I feel a stirring of excitement for the day ahead.

I never thought I'd have such concrete plans to play with myself or that I'd get paid for it, but here we are.

The thought of work brings to mind X-rated images featuring a certain someone's intense blue eyes and stern mouth.

I fight the sudden urge to reach down and explore the newly bare skin near my clit. My orgasms belong to the project at the moment.

With a sigh, I hug my pillow and drift off to sleep.

Chapter Five

*I*n the morning, I feed Monkey and check my work email as I eat an omelet.

"You better be good." I jokingly frown at my guinea pig as I collect my work laptop, work phone, and the suitcase. "I'm about to spank the monkey."

She looks at me with a blank expression.

"What, you think *monkey* is supposed to represent a cock in that phrase?" I ask her.

No reaction.

"I know, right? Why are so many animals used as a euphemism for genitals in the first place? Cat, rooster, monkey—does humanity have a subconscious bestiality streak?"

She turns on her heel and scurries into her house again—clearly not interested in dignifying my words with a response.

I carry the work phone, the laptop, the suitcase, and Precious into the bedroom, then light a few candles around the bed and play Leonard Cohen on my Echo to set the mood.

Opening the suitcase, I take out the vibrator, the toy I've been most curious about—mostly because Ava has been singing praises of hers so much I suspect she gets a commission from the manufacturer.

This specific vibrator is made of some squishy Space Age material that feels like a jelly made out of slugs—but sexy pink, so I guess it's okay.

I already have my first quality complaint: the vibrator box doesn't have any instructions on it, nor is there a little paper manual inside. There's only one short note on the box: *Get the Belka app for your phone.*

I make a note of this in my testing document. It's feasible the Belka peeps omitted more instructions because these are prototypes, but unlikely. The packaging is too polished for that, so this might well be an oversight.

Hopefully, my Bachelor of Science degree will help me figure out how to use a vibrator, even a smart one.

I get the app onto Precious and choose "Vibrator" from the screen with the different toy options. The app informs me that it's connected to the vibrator via Bluetooth, and that the vibrator's battery is full—a great start.

I click on the "Connect with Partner" icon and learn that you can do so via email, text, or even social media.

I opt to test the text version for now and put in the number of my work phone.

To make it seem like I'm testing the toys over the internet, I set up my work phone to connect through a proxy server located in Tajikistan—the farther, the better. Then I click on the text and am directed to download the Belka app. Once the app is ready to go, it opens up a small videoconference window—with options to see/hear your partner or not.

I document all this.

The setup was pretty effortless. Then again, it might be good to have someone less tech-savvy play with all this just in case—perhaps someone's adventurous granny?

In any case, the work phone version of the app is now in "Giver" mode, while Precious is the "Receiver."

I leave only the work phone in my hands because I need the controls on it. They consist of a start button and the knob for intensity.

First things first. I apply the vibrator to my forearm and press start.

Wow.

It's not just vibrating. The strange material makes it ripple, for lack of a better term. It feels... interesting. I play with the intensity until I find one that I suspect will feel good on my clit, then stop the vibrator.

Hiking up the skirt of my dress, I pull down my panties. Just for shits and giggles, I'm wearing the gag

44

pair Ava got me after my breakup. They boldly state "Open for Business."

Carefully, I press the vibrator to myself. It feels tickly and a little cold.

Here we go. Time to start my workday.

I open the timer app for the "Duration" section of the testing document and reach for the start button.

Precious pings, stopping me.

Swapping the work phone for personal, I see that I just got a text from Ava.

Figures. Is it considered cockblocking when someone prevents you from using a vibrator?

When you get around to the toys, think of being impaled by the Impaler, her text states.

How did she sniff out what I'm about to do? She must've used her own vibrator so much she's gained a psychic superpower. Or maybe she was bitten by her vibrator—by its Bluetooth, perhaps?

Precious pings again. This time, it's the eggplant emoji.

I'm busy, I reply and silence Precious before grabbing the work phone once more.

As my finger hovers over the start button, I do my best to thwart Ava by not thinking of the Impaler.

Riiight. As everyone who's ever tried *not* to think of something knows, the more you try, the more you end up thinking of the forbidden object.

And that's doubly so for when said object is as hot as the one I have in my mind's eye.

Fine. Whatever. I might feel better if I picture yummy lips touching my clit instead of slug jelly.

The image of hypnotic lapis lazuli eyes firmly in my head, I set a timer and press the start button.

Bzzz.

I drop both the phone and the vibrator as a powerful orgasm unleashes a wave of endorphins into my system. A full-on, toe-curling orgasm—as amazing as it was unexpected.

As the last spasms ripple through my body, I stare at the toy dumbfounded.

Did that just happen?

Is this a military grade vibrator, or did I just develop the female counterpart to premature ejaculation?

Chewing on my lip, I open the laptop and look at the testing document.

"Was orgasm achieved?" You can say that again.

"How many times?" Once so far.

"Session duration?" No clue. I put down a microsecond.

What now? Maybe I do the same test one more time? After all, whoever put the handwritten notes together implied there would be multiple sessions.

When I attempt it, I grunt in pain instead of pleasure. My clit is super-sensitive from the last go.

I might have to give it a little break.

With some trepidation, I snatch the dildo from the suitcase and open the packaging.

Again no instructions, just a small packet of lube

and the thing itself—huge and made of the same squishy material as the vibrator, only avocado-green instead of pink.

I don't mention this in my work report, but this thing reminds me of an alien tentacle. I mentally dub it Glurp.

Taking Glurp in my hand, I uncharitably compare him to my exes' equipment.

Yup, Glurp is a big boy, almost frighteningly so.

Opening the lube, I nearly drown Glurp in the viscous liquid and bring up the mental image of the Impaler as I slide the tip into my opening.

Hmm.

It fits and feels kind of nice already. The prior orgasm must've gotten me ready for this.

I push Glurp deeper and pick up the work phone to bring the tentacle to life.

Bzzz.

I don't instantly come this time, but the vibration or whatever it's doing feels amazing. My inner muscles tighten, and I feel like I'm on the verge of something truly intense.

A few interesting options show up on the app, like A-spot and G-spot stimulation.

I'll have to test them all, but for now, I decide on the G-spot because it's the one I've actually heard about.

I jab my finger at the G-spot button.

Glurp begins to lightly twist inside me, as if zooming in on a target.

Bing-bing.

The videoconferencing app on my work phone hides part of the Belka app screen.

Crap. It's Sandra, my boss.

What the hell does she want? There's micromanaging, and then there's interrupting your loyal employee from finding Nemo.

I stab the screen to reject the call.

The videoconferencing app expands to full screen.

Oh, shit.

I must've fat-fingered it.

"Hi, Fanny." Sandra's eyes widen. "Am I interrupting something?"

I redden like a boiled crab and swiftly disable the video.

Did she see anything? Can't be—the camera was aimed at my face, not at Glurp.

At least I hope it was.

But then why the question? Maybe she figured something was up by the blissed-out look on my face?

"I just wanted to make sure Project Belka is on track," Sandra says apologetically, and I realize I haven't responded to her still.

"Don't worry about a thing," I half say, half squeal. "It's in good hands."

I have no idea if she hears or responds because at that moment, Glurp finally gives my G-spot a knockout.

I bite my cheek to prevent a moan from escaping as my eyes roll back in my head.

"Thanks," Sandra says. "Email an update when you get the chance."

"Yes!"

She hangs up.

I extricate Glurp from myself and rush into the bathroom to splash some icy water on my overheated face. Leaving Glurp behind to be cleaned, I get back and record this session in the document.

They better allow me to move departments. After today, I can never work for Sandra again, or look her in the eye.

Also, can one develop a fetish this way? Next thing I know, I'll need Sandra to call me every time I get hot and heavy.

Looking into the suitcase, I debate what to test next.

The buttplug catches my attention.

It's small enough not to be intimidating—a good thing for me, a butt play virgin.

I take the package out and read the title.

Anal Belka.

Does Belka mean something besides the name of this project?

A quick search reveals that Belka is actually a common word in various Slavic languages. It means *beam* in Polish (ouch), *egg white* in Macedonian (weird), and *squirrel* in Russian (hmm, okay). Given Vlad's country of birth, I have to assume the title of both the toy and the project means the latter.

In which case... an anal squirrel? Sounds like a

rodent obsessed with keeping his park nice and tidy. Who decided that was a good name for this thing?

Then again, Ava told me about the time they had a guy come to the ER with a hamster stuck in his butt —so rodents in butts must be something people are interested in doing. Why not a squirrel, too?

I can never tell Monkey about this. As a rodent herself, she'll be scarred for life. At least in the case of this Belka, no animals need to be harmed.

Placing the work phone on the bed, I lie on my stomach and squirt the lube that came with the squirrel toy into my butt.

The things I do for science.

Or quality assurance.

Or a paycheck.

Feeling naughty, I place the tip of the toy at my opening and push lightly to see how much resistance my body provides. There's some, but not as much as I expected.

Well, okay, the squirrel *is* small.

I get bolder and increase the pressure.

There's a small hint of discomfort, and then, like a baster into a turkey, the squirrel dives right in.

Chapter Six

*W*hoa. That feels strange. But also kind of good, maybe? I can't decide.

I set the timer on the phone and load "Anal Belka" as the toy on the app.

A few new controls appear on the screen that weren't available in the case of the vibrator and Glurp. For example, there's a button named "Out" and one named "Deeper."

I'm not ready for deeper just yet, and out is premature.

I press "On."

The squirrel begins to vibrate.

The feeling is odd, but not unpleasant. As I adjust, I feel ready to brave more, and a button that says "P-spot stimulation" catches my gaze.

I've never heard of a P-spot. Then again, I've never heard of the A-spot either. To be honest, I didn't even know there were "spots" in the backdoor area, but I guess there must be since so many women like butt play.

I hesitantly press on the P-spot button.

The squirrel stops vibrating and gently burrows deeper into me.

Weird.

It keeps moving.

Wait a second.

It stops. I feel it whirling around as if looking for something, then it starts moving again.

What the hell? I jab the stop button.

Nothing happens. The squirrel continues on its merry way.

I frantically press the out button.

The squirrel stops.

Whew.

Wait a second. The squirrel is whirling around again, as if rooting for something inside me. Not finding whatever it is, it burrows even deeper.

What the fuck? Does "P" stand for pancreas? I think that's an organ in the digestive system, but there's no way that's a fun spot.

I scan the screen in panic.

There's a help button here, plus a few more that don't look promising.

I punch all the non-help buttons at once.

The squirrel keeps going deeper.

I'm beginning to freak out. What if "P" stands for the pituitary gland in the brain?

The squirrel stops. An error pops up on the screen, stating, "Prostate not found."

Prostate? Oh, no. Women don't have one—at least not in the butt area. There's something called Skene's glands on the front side of the vagina that are sometimes referred to as "the female prostate," but that's clearly not what the squirrel was looking for.

Through my panic, I begin to parse out what happened. The squirrel must be from the batch meant for the male sex. When the Impaler wrote the app, he forgot to account for a situation where someone who wants P-spot stimulation lacks a prostate to stimulate.

It's not a surprising bug, but it *is* a major pain in my ass—and that expression has never been this literal.

I swipe angrily at the error message until it disappears from the screen. Then I pound the out button.

The error comes back, and nothing else happens.

Out of options, I click the help button again.

A sound resembling a dial tone emanates from the phone.

That's not good. I bet that's meant to dial customer service when Belka toys get into the hands of real customers. This early, I doubt anyone's going to answer that call. Not that I'd know what to tell them if they did.

Frantic, I drop the work phone on the bed and grab Precious to dial Ava.

"I'm a little busy," she says in lieu of a hello.

"This is a medical emergency! Code red. I'm not joking, this is——"

"Whoa, slow down, slow down. What happened?"

"I have a squirrel stuck in my rectum. Or maybe my colon. Somewhere up there."

A moment of silence, then: "Is this a joke?"

"I wish! I was testing the toys and——"

Ava sounds like she's got something stuck in her throat. "So the squirrel is a toy?"

"No, I mean a real fucking animal."

"Hey, you never know. I've heard of lots of things stuck in there. Fruits, vegetables, keys, candles, coffee and peanut butter jars, lightbulbs, deodorant, smart-phones, bottles of body spray, Buzz Lightyear——"

"That's not making me feel any better." I squeeze the phone tighter. "What should I do?"

"Go to the ER," she says.

"How about something less drastic," I say, picturing how embarrassing such a trip would be—especially since my name is Fanny.

For the rest of their lives, the nurses would tell everyone, "The patient's name was Fanny, and she had a toy stuck in her fanny."

Ava takes an audible breath. "Do you have any abdominal pain?"

"No."

"How about bleeding?"

All blood drains from my face. "This just happened. You think there could be bleeding?"

"Unlikely, if there's no pain. Just make sure not to

reach in there with tongs or anything that could cut or bruise the area. That includes your nails."

I squeeze my eyes shut. "I'm not an idiot. At least not more of an idiot."

"Okay, but just keep in mind: There are cases where tongs have gotten stuck along with the original object."

"No tongs," I say firmly. "What can I do, though?"

"Other than going to the ER? You can try to poop it out."

I feel a pang of hope. "You think that would work?"

"If it's small enough, it should come out the way it came in."

I look at the empty box from the toy. "How small is small enough?"

"I have no idea. Did it go in easy?"

My face reddens. "Kind of."

"Then maybe it'll be a case of easy come, easy go."

Ugh. "This isn't funny!"

"Look, I've really got to run. Keep me posted. If you decide to go to the ER, come here, to Presbyterian."

I grimace. "I'm trying the poop method first."

"Eat some fiber," she says. "Better yet, a laxative."

With that useful advice, she hangs up.

As I place Precious back on the bed, I see something on the work phone that chills my bones.

The help call looks to have connected somewhere.

"Hello?" I squeak into the receiver. "Is someone there?"

"Ms. Pack," says a familiar, Russian-accented voice. "I strongly disagree with your plans and am on my way to take you to the ER immediately."

Chapter Seven

"*No*, don't! I'll call 911. Don't come here!"

No reply. He hung up.

Growling in frustration, I click the help button again.

A sound resembling a dial tone emanates from the phone once more, but when I wait and wait, it doesn't connect anywhere.

Maybe I can call him directly?

Sure. Just as soon as I magically figure out what his cell phone number is. Unless… maybe Sandra knows?

Ugh, no. I don't want her involved. She'll either have a heart attack from thinking the project has gone awry, or from laughter when she learns what's happened.

How does the Impaler even know where I live? Did the app access the work phone GPS, or did he simply take a look at my employee file?

Anyway, the how is not important. The fact that he's going to be here is. It's bad enough he overheard the whole "squirrel in my butt" conversation with Ava —a fact that makes me want to crawl into a ditch and die. If he comes here and needs to rescue my ass— literally—I might just melt from mortification.

There's only one thing to do.

I must poop out the squirrel.

Having a clear-cut goal feels good, so I cautiously stand up.

Still no abdominal pain, so that's good. Unfortunately, the squirrel doesn't start moving down with the pull of gravity—on some level, I was hoping it might.

Fine.

I shuffle to the bathroom with a stiff gait. So this is why they call this style of locomotion "having something stuck up the butt."

I get on the toilet and wait.

Nothing happens.

I strain.

Nada.

After a few minutes of pointless waiting, I recall Ava talking about fiber. Getting up, I stiffly shuffle into the kitchen and grab an apple.

Crunching it, I return to my white throne.

Nope.

Oh, who am I kidding? I know fiber needs more than minutes to do its thing.

Getting up, I try pacing the apartment.

Doesn't help.

I roll out my yoga mat and do a Standing Forward Bend.

Not even a little stomach cramp.

Doing other poses doesn't work either—neither the Downward-Facing Dog, nor the Triangle, nor the Seated and Supine Twists.

Monkey watches me do all this with an unreadable expression.

"Don't judge," I tell her and prepare for the big guns: the Wind-Removing Pose, where you're on your back and your knees touch your chest.

Even this mighty yoga weapon doesn't work.

Okay. I need to be ready for the eventuality of seeing the Impaler—and I'm a mess in ways beyond foreign objects in my rear end.

I quickly change my drab casual dress for a prettier one, grab my makeup kit and a mirror, and perch on the toilet (hope springs eternal) to make myself look semi-human.

Lipstick is easy. Lashes too. But no matter how hard I work on the missing eyebrow, I fail to make it look like the sister of the other—barely a second cousin is the best I can do.

Maybe I should get rid of the remaining one right now? Problem is, I don't own a razor, and I don't dare play with the hair removal cream under the current circumstances. The last thing I want is to end up with bald spots on my head or hair removal cream in my butt. Or worse.

The eyebrow situation adds to my frustration.

Who does he think he is, coming here like this?

Well, I guess he thinks he's my boss squared. Probably realizes that having the power to fire me allows him to do what he wants. Probably doesn't like the sound of the lawsuit my parents would file if I somehow died because of the squirrel. Still—

The doorbell rings, sending my pulse through the stratosphere.

He's here!

Even the prospect of the upcoming humiliation doesn't loosen anything up—so much for stories of people soiling themselves out of fear. Then again, there's also a conflicting "anus clenching in fear"—so maybe that's what's happening here?

My work phone rings. Then Precious joins in.

Feeling like I'm about to die, I answer.

"How are you feeling?" the Impaler asks.

I gulp. Is that genuine concern in his voice? "Never better. You didn't need to come. I got this—"

"We're going to the ER." The statement is a command with no room for negotiation. "Do you need help coming out?"

Am I hearing a threat in that question? Will he break my door down if I answer the wrong thing?

Nah. His kind need to be officially invited to enter someone's home.

I rub my burning cheeks. "I can walk."

"See you soon then." He hangs up.

I text Ava an update, grab both phones, shuffle over to the door, and put on a pair of sneakers.

Here goes nothing.

I open the door.

He's here, in all his mouthwatering glory.

He meets my gaze, and something—probably shame—makes my knees go weak.

His strong hand grasps my elbow.

Electricity shoots up my arm from his touch, and I nearly stumble.

His expression changes, a scowl appearing on his face. He yells something in Russian, and a burly middle-aged dude is suddenly holding my other elbow with sausage-like fingers that are hairier than those of a sasquatch.

He came with a minion?

"Step carefully," the Impaler instructs.

When I put one foot in front of the other without faceplanting, he grunts approvingly.

Reluctantly accepting their help, I let them lead me to a limo that's waiting at the curb.

They open the door and deposit me inside. The Impaler climbs in to sit next to me. I catch a faint whiff of his yummy bergamot and citrus scent, and my breathing turns fast and shallow.

I hope I don't faint. Who knows what could come out of me if I do?

The minion gets behind the wheel and slams the door behind himself.

I clear my suddenly dry throat. "So, you have a chauffeur?"

The Impaler leans over and secures me with a

seatbelt—nearly causing my brain to melt in the process. "Ivan is more what you'd call a personal assistant."

Really? Ivan looks more like a bodyguard, or that mobster guy who wanted to chop the yellow M&M into little bits and sprinkle them on ice cream in that Super Bowl ad.

Ivan's expression is grim as he turns the key in the ignition.

Could he be *the* Ivan, as in The Terrible? I can picture it now: The Impaler was feeling lonely, found a man with a name almost as grandiose as his own, turned him, and began a beautiful friendship.

With a squeal of tires, the car torpedoes forward.

"We're going to Presbyterian, right?" I ask when I swallow my heart back into my chest.

The Impaler closes the partition, separating us from Ivan. "Your friend sounded like she knew what she was talking about."

As I recall the conversation he's referring to, a wave of tingling heat hits my face.

Without paying much attention to me, he picks up a laptop from the neighboring seat and pops it open to a page filled with stylish lines of code.

His eyes narrow on the screen, and those lickable fingers dance over the keyboard with the grace of a pianist.

"Give me the phone that's in Giver mode," he says without looking up.

As I hand him my work phone, I get an inkling of

what he's doing, and fleetingly debate jumping out of the car.

After a few minutes of typing, he attaches the phone to his laptop's USB and drums his fingers on the trackpad as he waits for something—my guess is for the app to update.

"Say something if you feel anything," he says and clicks a button on the screen, confirming my suspicion.

Somewhere inside me, the squirrel comes to life.

"Something!" I redden to boiled lobster levels.

He nods approvingly and clicks something else, putting the squirrel back to sleep.

"You fixed the bug I found," I say, voicing my earlier theory.

"It was a good find." He looks right at me as he says this. "Great job."

My heart flutters pleasantly in my chest. If I were always complimented on my testing like this, I might not want to switch to the development department.

Reddening more, I reach for the phone in his hand. "Let's stop at the nearest bathroom, and I'll take care of the rest."

"No." He yanks the device out of my reach. "I've done some research. You need an X-ray and a doctor's supervision."

He did research on things to do when your employee has an object stuck in her fanny?

Someone shoot me. It would be a mercy killing.

The car comes to a jerky stop.

"We're here," he says, leaning in to unbuckle my seatbelt.

My hormones go into overdrive.

Stop it. He's your boss squared.

But he smells so yummy.

Now you sound like a cannibal. Get a grip. He—

"Are you okay?" he asks.

"Peachy." Was that concern again? More importantly, how long was I talking to myself?

"Let's go." He guides me out. Then he and his personal assistant grab an elbow each and lead me into the ER entrance like an invalid.

Hey, it could've been worse. He could've wheeled over a wheelchair. Or a gurney.

Leaving me in the waiting room, my boss squared sends Ivan back to the car and goes to get forms from the check-in desk—which gives me a moment to shoot a text to Ava to let her know that I'm here.

I'll come see you, she replies. *Wait there.*

Sure. I was so going to prance away before, but now I'll wait.

Coming back with the forms, the Impaler helps me fill them out—as though my fingers are damaged. Midway, we have an argument: Instead of letting me use insurance, the very same one his company provides me with, he wants to pay for everything himself.

"I made you come here," he says over my objections. "It's the least I can do."

Fine. He did drag me here. Let him pay—and I'm

sure the bill will be huge enough to teach him a lesson about people's free will.

"Fanny!" Ava is wearing her scrubs and grinning like a loon. Her eyes dart between me and my boss squared.

"I'm going to hand in the forms," the Impaler says after I introduce them.

Ava waits until he's (hopefully) out of earshot before she jumps up and down and claps her hands like a preschooler. "You didn't tell me the Impaler looked like *that*. And he brought you here? Did the two of you—"

"Is there a private room where you can hide me?" I glance over to see how far away the Impaler is—and it's a good thing I do, because he's coming back.

"Not officially, but yeah," Ava says. "First, I'll take you for an X-ray."

Catching the end of that sentence, the Impaler nods approvingly.

Ava quirks an eyebrow. "Mr. Chortsky, would you like to wait here, go to Fanny's room, or come with us for the X-ray?"

I glare at her. I don't want him anywhere near my room. Or my X-ray.

He grabs my elbow again—sending another wave of tingles through me. "I'm going with."

Ava winks at me before she helps him lead me to the service elevator, which she opens with her hospital ID.

A corridor later, she ushers me into the room

where a technician awaits. I cast a worried glance at her and the Impaler, who hang back together in the hallway.

I have a bad feeling about this, and not just because it makes me jealous. Ava doesn't have much of a filter when she speaks, so who knows what damage she might do?

Since I don't have a choice, I do my best to make the X-ray process as fast as possible, and when I sprint out of the room, Ava and the Impaler stop mid-word.

Does she look guilty?

Before I can confront anyone, I'm led to a nearby nurse's station where Ava turns a screen our way.

On the screen is an X-ray that shows what one would expect: an image of a classically beautiful pelvis with a ghostly outline of the squirrel toy below a nicely shaped coccyx bone.

No wonder my parents always said I'm beautiful on the inside.

I catch the Impaler peering at the image with a deep frown, and I'm not sure how I should feel. On the one hand, he's seeing inside me—which is another level of embarrassing. On the other hand, there's definitely concern on his face, and even if it's due to fear of liability, it's still a sign that he kind of cares.

Still, I do wish he'd bought me a few dinners before I showed him my sacrum like this.

What are you saying? He can't get you dinners. Boss squared, remember?

"In light of this, your plan should work," Ava says to the Impaler.

I glare at her. "What plan?"

"The app." He waves the phone. "I can guide the—"

My glare moves to him. "You're not doing anything. If anyone's using that app, it's me."

Face unreadable, he hands me the phone. Our fingers brush again, and I feel a jolt of sensation that goes straight down to my core, reminding me of the orgasms I experienced just a short while ago.

Ava clears her throat. "Let's take you to your room."

I grumble as they lead me there, but nobody listens to me. When we arrive, Ava tells me to go in first so I can put on a robe.

I lock eyes with the Impaler. "You're staying out here—and that's final."

He inclines his head. "As you wish."

With an eye roll, I go inside and change.

Ava comes in a few seconds later and gestures for me to lie down on the bed.

When I'm horizontal, she hands me a bedpan. "Good call asking him to wait outside," she says, grinning hugely.

Muttering unintelligible curses, I put the bedpan under my rear end.

With a wink, Ava nods at the nearby defibrillator. "You think you're going to make it?"

Ignoring her, I click the out button on the app and hold my breath.

The squirrel comes to life once more and slowly, almost anticlimactically, begins to back out of its hiding spot.

It doesn't hurt at all, and if it weren't for the indignity of it all, I might even find the associated sensations a little interesting.

There's a moment of discomfort as the squirrel clears my opening, followed by a loud clang as the darn thing lands in the bedpan.

Giggling, Ava puts on a pair of latex gloves, snatches the bedpan, and dumps its contents into a biohazard bag.

"Seriously?" I ask.

She ceremoniously extends the bag to me. "When we remove bullets, we let people keep those too."

I jump off the bed and take a few steps.

"Feeling spry?" she asks.

I grab the bag, toss it into a garbage disposal labeled "Biohazard," and begin to change in sullen silence.

Ava refuses to leave it alone. "Do you want me to at least email you the X-ray? Or send it to him perhaps?"

I round on her. "Do that, and I'll smother you in your sleep."

Her eyes gleam with mischief. "So you like him a lot."

"Hush!" I hiss, cutting my eyes toward the door. "What if he's eavesdropping?"

She dramatically fans herself. "What a scandal."

I finish dressing and come toward her. Leaning in, I whisper, "Did he say anything about me when I was getting that X-ray?"

"Depends what you mean. He basically outlined the app solution and asked if that's safer than what a doctor would've done. No declarations of undying love, though."

"Well, good," I say, hiding my disappointment. "Let's go."

I stride out of the room, Ava on my heels.

The Impaler's deep blue eyes zero in on my face. "Did it work?"

The redness that had managed to leave my cheeks during the squirrel removal procedure returns with a vengeance. "All good. The hardware is toast, though. I hope the Belka people can provide another."

"Don't worry about any of that." He adjusts his horn-rimmed glasses—a theoretically unsexy gesture that his fingers somehow turn erotic. "How do you feel?"

"Like getting *Exit Only* tattooed on my left butt cheek," I blurt, then redden painfully.

His expression is unreadable, his demeanor as aloof as ever. Ava, however, looks positively gleeful. "Make that a tramp stamp."

I glare at her.

"Actually, that might not work as intended," the

Impaler says, his tone utterly serious. "Some may take it as a challenge."

Oh. My. God. Does he realize what he just said?

Ava makes a choking sound as I hustle to the elevator, determined to hide my flaming face.

We ride down in silence, and as I stare at the Impaler's implacable face, a new worry invades my mind.

What happens now that the squirrel is out of me, and the emergency is over?

Am I about to lose my job?

Chapter Eight

I try to parse that indecipherable expression of his.

Is he angry about what happened? Is that why he told me not to worry about any of it? Are my days of testing toys—or anything—over?

It's possible. I doubt any other employee has interrupted his day like this, and made him drive them to the hospital.

Then again, my snafu did help locate a possible bug in his code, so that's something. Unless he's like Britney—touchy about the flaws in his app.

Oh, well. Even if he does want to fire me, I bet he wouldn't do that right after I've been rushed to a hospital—it wouldn't look so good if I decided to sue.

Which I wouldn't, but he doesn't know that.

The elevator doors slide open.

"See you," Ava says to me when we exit. Turning

to the Impaler, she adds, "Thanks for taking care of her. Nice to have met you."

He inclines his head, and she sprints away.

We check out of the hospital and leave the building.

Ivan is waiting inside the car.

The Impaler opens a door for me in a gentlemanly fashion, and I climb in, making sure to plop on the seat opposite to where his laptop is. I don't think it's wise for me to sit next to him after all of this.

I might expire from blushing.

Before he decides to buckle me in again, I do that myself—same reason.

He takes a seat next to his laptop, as I hoped he would, but for some reason, I feel a pang of disappointment.

Ivan floors the gas pedal.

The Impaler raises the partition between us and his minion, and glances at his laptop before pinning me with an intent stare.

Crap. I'm probably interrupting him from something important.

"So..." I shift in my seat uncomfortably. "What now?"

He cocks his head. "We're taking you home, of course."

Since it's been whole minutes since I last blushed, I do so now. "I meant, testing-wise." Or put another way, do I still have a job?

"You need to rest."

He's really good at making statements that sound like military orders. At least I don't salute or yes-sir him this time.

"How about after I rest?" I dare to ask.

"You're not going to worry about that right now."

That again. Should I just ask him straight out if I still have a job? Or will that just put the idea in his head?

"You went to Brooklyn College, right?" he asks out of nowhere.

"I did." Wait. How does he know? Did he notice it in my file when he looked for my address?

"Great computer science program," he says. "Soothing campus."

I blink at him. "How do you know? Are you a fellow alum?"

"Guilty." Something almost like a smile touches the corners of his eyes. "I graduated eight years before you, so our paths never crossed."

Huh. So he did look up my file, even down to the date of my graduation.

I wonder what it would've been like if we'd met in school and he weren't my boss squared.

Are you crazy? Who says he's even attracted to you? He's just giving you a ride home, followed by a possible job termination.

I moisten my dry lips. "Did you also major in comp sci?"

Did his gaze just fall to my mouth?

"What else?" he asks, the corners of his lips tilting

slightly—a definite smile, and a panty-wetting one at that.

"History," I blurt—and thank goodness don't add, "That would be easy for you, since you lived it."

His lips stretch into a full-blown smile. "No, I've been into programming forever. My older brother got me into it." He tilts his head. "How about you? Why did you choose that as your major?"

"It was an act of rebellion at first," I admit. "My parents are hippie-artsy types. They hoped I'd major in something like music, photography, or film— nothing practical, like computer science."

He arches an eyebrow. "There are other practical disciplines out there."

"Sure. I took a bunch of introductory STEM courses first, but something about programming appealed to me. Also, an asshole in that class didn't think I, a girl, could do it—which spurred me on."

At the mention of the asshole, the Impaler frowns deeply. Maybe it wasn't HR behind the women-to-men ratio, after all?

"The irony is," I continue, "writing code feels like that creative process that my parents yammer about all the time."

The frown relaxes. "Programming can be as much art as science."

I smile. "Just don't tell my parents that."

"I wouldn't dream of it," he says with mock seri-ousness. "Let them suffer knowing their daughter got herself a degree that will virtually guarantee she's always got a well-paying job, and one that will likely intellectually stimulate her as well. The horror."

My smile widens. "What did *you* like about computer science when you tried it?"

He adjusts his glasses again. "I liked the logic and certainty of it. In other sciences, there are a lot of theories which may or may not be the ultimate truth. In ours, most theories have proofs, like in math. I also like the feeling of control when I code. With computers being as prevalent as they are, not knowing how to program, or at least how it all works, is a little like not knowing how to read and—"

His phone rings, distracting us both, and I realize I was listening openmouthed—in part because I got drawn in by the passion in his voice. If being a super-rich company owner ever gets boring, he can always do inspirational speaking on the side.

He glances at the screen of his phone but doesn't pick up. "Where was I?"

Crap. Did he just ignore something important because of me? "It's fine," I say. "You should take that."

He pockets the phone. "You said your parents are into art. What do they do for a living?"

His phone rings again.

He ignores it, his gaze trained expectantly on me.

Would it be rude if I insist that he pick that up and therefore ignore the question?

Sensing my reluctance, he takes out the phone and pointedly silences it.

"Mom is an opera singer," I say after the phone disappears into his pocket again. "Dad's a painter."

He looks fascinated. "Does she perform somewhere, and does he have exhibits?"

"Mom mostly teaches others, but Dad did finally get famous enough to be able to sell his works. That happened just as I was graduating from college. When I was growing up, our income was pretty low—full-ride financial aid for college kind of low."

"I also got that," he says to my surprise. "When we arrived in this country, we didn't have an income at all."

Ah, yes, of course. Immigrant background. "Your parents must be proud of what you've accomplished."

"Take it for granted, more like." He frowns again. "I think they feel like they gave up their lives back in Russia for their kids, so their standards for what's considered a worthy accomplishment are out of control."

"Well, at least they didn't name you Fanny when your last name is Pack," I say, eager to rid him of that frown. "As you can imagine, I was the butt of a lot of jokes. Pun intended."

My evil plan works. Another smile touches the corners of his eyes. "I think I would prefer parents with a sense of humor—even if it meant I'd end up named after an accessory."

"That's because you don't know my parents. You know how teens are embarrassed by their parents? I've felt that way my whole life. They're completely inappropriate. For example, they had 'the birds and the bees' talk with me when I was five—with diagrams and everything."

Another real smile graces his lips. "Better than never—as was the case with mine."

I want to trace the curve of those sexy lips with my finger. *No, stop it, perv. Boss squared, remember?* With effort, I return my focus to the conversation at hand. "Still, you've never been to middle school with my name," I say.

He's unfazed. "My last name, Chortsky, means 'from a chort'—which is Russian for 'demon.' Chort is also a popular curse word, kind of like 'damn.'"

Huh. So it's official, he *is* evil. Still, poor guy. I picture a little boy with that name, being teased unmercifully. "At least your parents didn't choose that name," I say. "They suffered with it too."

He shrugs. "They could've changed it."

"Fine, you win—if it's a win to have parents worse than mine." I cock my head. "What do they do?"

"Right now, they own a restaurant on Brighton Beach. In Russia, though, my father was a surgeon and my mother an architect."

Before I can ask anything else, the limo comes to a stop.

I glance out the window.

Wow. I didn't even notice the ride home.

"Go rest," he says, his commanding tone returning and the earlier smile gone without a trace.

I fight the urge to ask about testing again. Something tells me it wouldn't be welcome at this juncture.

"Bye," I say as I open the limo door.

"Until later, Ms. Pack." He pauses, then adds gently, "By the way... you might want to check on your eyebrow."

Chapter Nine

I burst into my bathroom and stare in the mirror.

Of course. The eyebrow I drew earlier is barely a shadow of itself, and that mixture of curious, suspicious, and skeptical expressions is on my face in full force.

Ugh. Could this day have gone any worse?

The entire time I was talking to him, he must've been staring at that eyebrow. No wonder there were some smiles. He must've been dying of laughter inside.

I take out Precious and order an indelible eyebrow pencil, eyebrow powder, and temporary eyebrow tattoos. I even splurge on stick-on human hair eyebrow wigs in the hopes that one of these things will let me look human again.

When my mortification subsides a little, I check my work email.

Empty inbox.

I've never had zero email before. Even on my first day with Binary Birch, a welcome message was waiting for me, as well as something from HR and Sandra.

Speaking of Sandra, I dial her up.

"You're supposed to be resting," she says instead of a hello.

"I am?" Did she say that sternly?

"I just got off the phone with Mr. Chortsky. He made his feelings clear."

I feel like I'm about to fall through the floor. "Did he explain why?"

"Mr. Chortsky, explaining himself to me?"

This time, I definitely detect a note of annoyance —hopefully at the Impaler and not me. "Look, Sandra, about the testing I was—"

"That's another thing." Her tone is clipped. "We're not to speak about Project Belka or any sort of work until you've rested—and once you have, he wants our interactions to happen face to face."

Weirder and weirder... unless they plan to fire me, that is. I think firing someone face to face is how it's usually done.

"Is there anything else I can help with? Some other projects I can work on?" I ask in desperation. "Being bored won't help me rest."

Sandra sighs. "What about your app? You can always work on that. The cleaner that code, the higher the chance it will impress people."

Is that a hint? Do I need to prepare a resume and use that app as my portfolio?

"Did you send a link to my code to the development department?" I ask, fishing for more hints on my fate.

"As soon as I got it," she says.

"And?"

"I haven't heard back from anyone yet. I'm sure the dev team will review it in due course."

Unless I'm fired. "Okay, thanks, Sandra. How about I swing by the office tomorrow, after I've rested for the remainder of today?"

"Is that what you and Mr. Chortsky discussed?"

"He didn't exactly define the word 'rest' for me, if that's what you mean."

She heaves another sigh. "Fine. As long as you've rested by then, I'm free at eleven tomorrow. Would that work for you?"

"Yep. See you then," I say and hang up before she can change her mind.

———

After I eat lunch and feed Monkey, I decide to do what Sandra said—check on my app source control repository.

A surprise is waiting for me there.

For the first time ever, someone is collaborating on the project with me.

The first message is about a bug report.

Actually, it's more than that. It's an unwelcome critique of the app as a whole—dripping with cattiness.

Quaint app. Not bad for someone who's never coded a day in her life. For your information, if you aim the app at an image of a cartoon character's face, the returned lookalike isn't the same character. So, for example, I used it on Daffy Duck, and your app decided he looks most like Donald Duck. If you think about it logically, Daffy looks most like Daffy.

Hmm. I bring up a picture of Daffy on my work phone and use Precious to aim my app at him. The app indeed says he looks like Donald instead of himself.

So this is a legit bug—especially if one forgets for a second that the app was made for people to use, not cartoon characters. At least a duck looks like a duck. If the app claimed Donald Duck looked like Bugs Bunny, that would be worse.

I check out the helpful user—screen name Crazy-Oops. No profile image, but the screen name itself is enough for me to guess who this is. First half must refer to *(You Drive Me) Crazy* and second half to *Oops!...I Did It Again*, both songs by Britney Spears.

I'd bet Monkey's liver this user is another Britney. As in, Britney Archibald. She must've been dying to find a bug in my code to retaliate for the numerous flaws I found in hers.

Hey, at least it means the development department got Sandra's email, and some of them are looking at my code. Maybe the others are less biased. In fact, I see a couple of other messages already.

First, though, I record CrazyOops's IP address. If she's made other accounts in order to further diss the app, I'll know it's her.

Surprisingly, the next message is not a bug report. Instead, someone located the reason the app was doing what Britney bitched about and fixed it.

Holy binary. Who is this mysterious do-gooder?

The screen name is Phantom, and the profile picture is of the half-masked face of the Phantom of the Opera.

That's not a lot to go by. Maybe she or he is someone who likes the classics—but that can be lots of people.

Putting aside the mystery of the identity of this person, I check out the next message from them.

It's not a bug report or a fix this time, just a direct message. A long one at that. In it, Phantom suggests a whole range of interesting and fun features for the app and includes references to open source projects and libraries that I can use to implement said features with relative ease.

Also, Phantom suggests a number of improvements that would "make the app ready for wide use." The issue that stands out to them is that my database of user pictures is public at the moment, which will cause privacy concerns with the more paranoid users. Here, too, Phantom suggests references that I can use to make this job easier.

I double-check the IP. Not the same as Britney's, but I could've guessed that based on the supportive tone and because she'd never end a message to me the way Phantom has:

Your code is elegant. I think you have a talent for this. Don't give up, and you'll go far.

Even though I have no idea who Phantom is, it's got to be someone on the dev team, which makes me swell with pride.

Also, I get the screen name now. Whoever this is, they're acting like a mentor, which the Opera Phantom was to Christine.

I just hope this Phantom isn't hideous, or harboring a dark obsession with me. Note to self: Don't call the Phantom an Angel of Software and keep an eye out for a mannequin that looks like me in a wedding dress.

Grinning, I write a thank-you message to the Phantom of the Code and spend the rest of the day familiarizing myself with all the sources they've provided me with.

As I work, I actually feel myself becoming a better programmer—or at least a cockier one.

When my eyes get tired, I log off and feed myself and my grumpy guinea pig some dinner. After that, I put on the gloves and the N95 mask again so I can rid myself of the one remaining eyebrow. I manage to do this without getting the toxic substance in my eyes, mouth, ears, or any other orifices.

Eyebrowless, I survey my pale face in the mirror. I look like I've gone through chemo, yet still better than when there was just one eyebrow.

Belatedly, I realize my big eyebrow-related shopping won't arrive in time for my meeting with Sandra. Oh well, I'll just draw them on and make sure to redraw as needed.

Thus determined, I finish my evening routine and go to sleep.

———

When I arrive in the office the next morning, Sandra and I grab the meeting room nearest her cube. She looks uncomfortable, exactly as I imagine she would if she were about to fire me.

Crap. Is this it?

"So," she says, steepling her fingers.

I brace myself. "Yes?"

"How are you?"

"Ready to work on something," I say, doing my best not to sound insubordinate.

She shifts in her seat. "The order from the top is that you're only to work on Project Belka."

I raise the patch of skin where I drew one of the eyebrows. "So I can just resume that?"

Sandra clears her throat. "Not until you've been deemed rested."

"Do I not look rested?" I take out a mirror and

make sure that I don't have bags under my eyes—and that the eyebrows are still in place.

She glances furtively in the vague direction of the Impaler's office. "I'm not the one who has to decide."

"I see." I drum my fingers on the desk. "So let me get this straight: I can't work on anything but the project that's on hold until I'm miraculously rested. And to top it off, if we want to talk about said project, it has to be face to face?"

She nods. "Sorry you ended up coming here for nothing. I was actually hoping you'd have an update for me."

Ah. She might be a little sore that I ended up interacting with her boss directly. She doesn't realize that was by accident.

I sigh. "I didn't mean to criticize *you*."

She gives me a slight smile. "I know. I'm sorry again that I got you into this mess in the first place. He wanted my best person on the project and—"

"Oh, don't worry. And thanks for passing along my code. I already got some feedback."

"That's great," she says. "From who?"

"They used screen names. But maybe you know… Is there anyone in the office who likes the Phantom of the Opera a little too much?"

She rubs her chin. "Rose, in accounting?"

Rose is pushing ninety, so if it's her, more power to her.

"My guess is that this is someone in the development department," I tell Sandra.

She frowns. "No one comes to mind."

"Okay, thanks." I stand up. "If that's all, I'm going to get some tea and head home."

"Good idea," she says. "My official directive to you is to rest."

"Got it." I give her the same crisp military salute I gave the Impaler, but this time as a joke.

She grins, and as we leave the room, she says, "My unofficial advice is to keep improving your coding skills."

Is that another hint about my fate? I almost ask outright, but I don't want to put her on the spot.

When I get to the pantry, I grab a chamomile packet and pour hot water into a cup.

Before I can dunk the tea bag into the water, I feel a presence enter the small room, creating a disturbance in the Force that gets my Spidey senses tingling.

As I look up, a pair of lapis lazuli eyes capture my gaze, making my stomach flutter.

"Ms. Pack," the Impaler says, his accent stronger than usual. "I hope I didn't startle you."

"Hi." The syllable comes out as a husky whisper that should be in an HR rulebook, filed under "inappropriate for the corporate environment."

"How do you feel?" He pours himself a cup of water.

I finally drop my chamomile packet into the water and pray that something about teabagging isn't about to escape my lips. "I feel ready for work again."

There. I can be appropriate when I focus very, very hard.

Speaking of, I shouldn't say the word *hard* either.

"Ready for work?"

It must be a Russian superpower to imbue such a short question with that much skepticism.

"Ready as a tropical storm." I lift my chin. "Isn't Project Belka urgent? You said that——"

"Not here." He frowns at the pantry entrance.

Sure enough, Britney is standing there, her eyes narrowed.

Was she a ninja in her past life?

"I understand," I say.

"Did you eat lunch yet?" he asks me.

I shake my head, struck mute by the question.

"In that case, it's my treat."

Taking my affirmative reply for granted, he strides toward Britney, whose eyes are catlike slits at this point.

For a second, I wonder if he'll be forced to tackle her.

But no. She moves out of the way.

As I hurry past her, I can feel a cloud of malevolence emanating from her, like poisonous mercury fumes. I don't have a chance to analyze it, though, because I'm overwhelmed by the realization that I'm going to lunch with the Impaler.

Me.

And him.

Eating together.

Like on a date?

No, that's stupid. This isn't a date. It's a work lunch, one that might be a ploy to fire me outside the office so I don't cause a scene.

Still. I feel giddy, like I'm going to prom—and I never actually went to prom.

Now I wish I were better dressed and had those premium human hair eyebrows glued on.

The Impaler stops by the elevator, and I'm so preoccupied with my thoughts that I slam into his back.

Holy cow. I just felt some seriously hard muscle.

Waving away my mumbling apology, he jabs the elevator button.

I stand there *not* thinking about licking his finger.

Nope.

Not me.

When the elevator doors open, he gestures for me to go first, so I do.

Realizing I'm still holding my tea, I gulp it down, the heat burning my insides. He mirrors me by downing his water in one go. His Adam's apple bobs up and down, and I want to lick it.

Stop fantasizing about licking random body parts.

His phone rings.

"Excuse me," he says and checks the screen.

Frowning at whatever message he's just received, he types out a reply with the speed a teenage girl would be proud of.

"Everything okay?" I ask when he looks up.

"Yes, but I only have fifty minutes for lunch. Is that okay?"

Even if it weren't okay, which it is, it's not like I'd tell him so. "You're a busy man. I understand."

We exit the building and cross the road, his long legs taking such wide strides I have to speed-walk to keep up.

Before I get sweaty, he stops next to a place I've never been to—because it's one of the best restaurants in New York City, and maybe the world. Or if not the best, then certainly the most expensive.

The Impaler pulls open the ornamental glass door. "After you."

Swallowing my awed disbelief, I step inside. As soon as the host sees the Impaler, he fawns over us as though we were royalty, leading us to a well-positioned table by the window—no doubt next to C-level executives of all the major corporations in the downtown area.

Boss squared must be a regular here.

Before I can say "nice to be in the top point-one percent," our glasses are filled with wine that no doubt costs more than I make in a year.

"Where's the menu?" I whisper, not wanting to sound like a rube to the nearby CEOs.

"I usually order the chef's choice," he replies, matching my lowered tone. "Want to risk it with me?"

Nodding, I take a sip of the amazing wine and check out the impeccable tablecloth in front of me.

This place is fancy. Too fancy to take someone if you wanted to fire them. Or just talk to them about testing sex toys, for that matter.

But then—

Can it be? Am I on a date?

Chapter Ten

*N*o. This can't be a date.

This is just a place he likes—and why not, if he can afford it? Since his parents own a restaurant, he's probably a major foodie and a snob for tablecloths and such.

Yeah. That must be it.

He scans my face. "Are you sure you're fine? You seem a little shell-shocked."

"It's this place, not the... umm... incident from yesterday," I reply, my cheeks instantly burning.

He looks around as if seeing the restaurant for the first time. "We could go somewhere else."

"No, this is fine. You've only got fifty minutes as is. I want to get down to business."

He arches his perfectly real eyebrow.

"Project Belka," I say. "I wanted—"

The waiter appears as if out of thin air and inquires if we've decided what to order.

"Chef's choice," we say in unison.

The waiter bows and scurries away.

"Back to the matter at hand." I take a sip of the wine, for bravery. "The testing for Project Belka—"

"Is not something we want to discuss in such a public venue." He glances at the swanky people nearby. "Wouldn't you agree?"

I put my wine glass down with a little too much force. "Isn't that why we're here?"

He gestures at the ice statues and the other décor. "We're here because we need to eat."

My cheeks flush, but with anger instead of embarrassment for a change. "I don't like having something like this hanging over me."

His sensuous lips flatten. "It doesn't have to."

Is that a threat? "So you're firing me over—"

"Firing you?" He looks genuinely perplexed. "Given the circumstances, I just assumed you'd want to give up the project."

I get it now. He doesn't think I can handle it. Like my asshole ex, he probably thinks I'm too much of a prude goody two-shoes for sex toys.

I'm so sick of this. Just because I have a round baby face that's prone to blushing, everyone makes these sweeping assumptions about me.

Fuck that.

"I'm not giving anything up. You'd have to pry the project from me. Is that clear?"

"Crystal." Amusement touches his eyes, but also something else—admiration maybe?

"I get that we can't talk details here," I say, switching to a tone that's much more appropriate when addressing my boss's boss. "Please pick a time and place that suits you. I'd really like to proceed with the project."

"Deal." He pulls out his phone and fires off a text. "How about this? If you come with me to my next engagement, we can talk in the limo on the way."

Next engagement? Before I can ask him for more details, the waiter arrives, carrying a small plate with something that looks like a crepe with caviar on it.

"De Jaeger," the waiter says. "And *kuznechik blinis*. The chef sends his regards to your father for the recipe."

So, my theory about his parents' restaurant having something to do with this lunch was correct.

This isn't a date.

Too bad. I was warming up to the idea.

"Care to explain what this is to this gourmet dummy?" I ask as soon as the waiter hurries away.

"Taste it first," he suggests.

I do, and an explosion of umami flavor tantalizes my taste buds. "Subtle nuttiness," I say in my best imitation of a posh food critic, "with the slightest hint of sweet, savory, and a note of woodiness."

"That's not a bad description," he says, tasting his portion.

"And what is it?"

He points at the white eggs. "That's snail caviar. And blinis are a type of Russian crepe, only instead of traditional buckwheat, these are made with cricket flour, which provides that nutty flavor."

Blood drains from my face.

To fight my gag reflex, I stay so silent you can hear crickets.

No. Must. Not. Think. Of. Crickets.

Or snails. Or slugs. Or the Blob. Or sentient snot. Or—

"This food is perfectly safe." The Impaler gives me a worried look. "You liked the way it tasted, didn't you?"

Well, yeah, but that was before I knew what abomination I was eating.

He waves at the waiter, who rushes over right away.

"The lady will have the chef's sampling of the children's menu," my boss squared declares.

The children's menu? So now he thinks that I'm not just unadventurous sexually, but also when it comes to food.

"No," I snap. "The lady will stick with the chef's choice."

The corners of the Impaler's mouth tilt up slightly as he asks the waiter, "What's coming next?"

"Balut Benedict," the waiter replies.

I nervously sip my wine. "That doesn't sound so bad."

"*Balut* is a duck egg in which the fetus has gotten a chance to develop into a little bird," the Impaler explains. "That Hollandaise sauce is usually made with duck eggs too."

"Fermented," the waiter adds helpfully.

Fermented.

Of course.

I didn't think my face could get any whiter, but there it is.

"I'm still sticking with it," I shock myself by saying. "What comes after the eggs?"

"Huitlacoche chowder," the waiter says, and I think he's beginning to enjoy himself at my expense.

The Impaler full-on smiles. "Huitlacoche is also known as corn smut—a fungus that used to destroy corn crops but nowadays is a delicacy."

"Seriously?" I look at the waiter.

He nods.

"I feel like I'm on the hidden camera version of Fear Factor," I say.

"You know what, I'll take the children's menu," the Impaler tells the waiter. His eyes gleam behind the lenses of his glasses as he asks me, "Want to join me?"

I sigh in defeat. "You don't need to do that."

"I insist. I've never tried the kids' menu, so I'm going to do it today."

"Fine." I take a small sip of my water, mostly to keep the crickets and the snail eggs down. "I'll have the children's menu too."

The waiter leaves.

The Impaler rightfully assumes the rest of the

crepes are all his, so he finishes them as I sit there, trying to think of how I can save face after all that.

Or at the very least, start some kind of a conversation.

My phone buzzes.

It's a text from Ava.

Impaled yet? This is followed by a syringe emoji and an eggplant.

It's like she sniffed out this maybe-date.

A burst of irritation at the world at large crystalizes into something more specific—namely, annoyance at Ava. I blurt out loud, "Who do you think would win in a fight: Snow White or Belle from *Beauty and the Beast*?"

There. It's more civilized than asking him if he thinks I'd succeed in pummeling Ava into the ground.

The Impaler swallows the last bite of his dubious appetizer, his forehead furrowing in thought. "Would this be a random encounter in a neutral location?"

"Why not?" I sip my wine, fighting the urge to push back that unruly lock of hair that keeps falling over his forehead.

It really, really wouldn't be appropriate.

The furrow underneath the lock of hair deepens. "We're talking standard versions of those characters?"

"There are versions?"

"Sure. The original story of *Beauty and the Beast* was French, but there's also a Russian one, which even has a cartoon that's much better than the Disney one —at least in my opinion. On the other hand, *Snow*

White was originally a story by Brothers Grimm. It also has a Russian version. She goes by Snowdrop and lives with seven *bogatyrs* instead of dwarves."

I lower my voice. "Is bogatyrs something disgusting they serve at this restaurant?"

He adjusts his glasses. "A bogatyr is a warrior from Russian legends."

I cock my head. "So this Russian Snow White lives with seven warrior dudes?"

He nods.

"That sounds like a reverse harem romance."

Amusement glimmers in the blue depths of his eyes. "I think she stays pure for her prince—who's not one of the 'dudes.' Also, the Disney version could be seen as reverse harem also, if your mind is dirty enough."

As someone whose mind is never far out of the gutter, I redden as I picture Sneezy, Grumpy, Dopey, and Sleepy in a gang bang with Snow White.

"How about we stick with Disney versions?" I say.

"In that case, Belle would win." He sounds as serious as if we were talking about the quarterly reports. "Of those two, Belle is more adventurous. She fought for the Beast at the end and had more depth when it came to her reasons for falling in love. In contrast, Snow White is a stereotypical damsel in distress who'd probably ask Prince Charming to fight Belle in her stead."

Damn it, he's right. I couldn't win even in this

allegorical battle—and what's worse, he just called my allegorical doppelgänger unadventurous.

The waiter comes back, carrying a tray filled with plates.

Everything looks safe enough, but I wait for him to explain what it is.

"Mixed yuca and yam fries in bechamel sauce," he says, pointing at the relevant plate. "Bluefin tuna fish sticks. Quail nuggets. Beaufort D'Été quesadillas."

I beam at the waiter in relief. "It all sounds delicious."

When he leaves, I lean toward the Impaler. "That's the kid's menu? Do they even allow children in this place?"

Another hint of a smile. "I've never seen one—and I'm a regular."

Figures.

I reach for one of the fries, and he must've had the same idea because our fingers touch.

I suddenly feel a hunger that has nothing to do with food.

"After you." He gestures at the fries.

I snatch a couple and stuff them into my mouth.

Wow.

Not sure if I got a yuca or a yam, but it's yum. The fish stick I try next is the best I've ever tasted, the nugget is pretty amazing as well, and when I bite into the quesadilla, I almost moan in pleasure.

Then I notice something. He's using a fork and a

knife for the items I've just eaten with my fingers, like a cavewoman.

I spear the next nugget with a fork. "This is much better than snail eggs."

"I'm glad, Ms. Pack. I wouldn't want you to regret my choice of this restaurant."

I chew the nugget, debating if I should ask him this or not. Finally, I decide to just go for it. "Look, after the hospital thing and this lunch, would you mind calling me Fanny?"

That way, I'll be able to stop thinking of round, hungry things and, more importantly, might forget for a moment that I'm lusting after my boss's boss.

His sexy lips quirk. "Fanny," he murmurs, and hearing my name with that accent makes me like it for the first time in my life. "Call me Vlad, then."

My heartbeat speeds up. "Vlad," I repeat obediently.

Wait, did that sound too husky? Because I really like the sound of his name on my lips. No more boss squared or the Impaler business for me. I'm calling him Vlad every chance I get.

Another smile curves his lips. "But no diminutives, okay?"

I blink at him. "Isn't Vlad already a diminutive form of Vladimir?"

He looks impressed. "I'd call it the short form, but that's pretty good for a non-Russian."

A warm glow spreads through me at his praise. "I picked up a few things in Brooklyn College. A high percentage of the computer science students shared your background. One guy called me Fan'ka, so I looked into this."

A dark gleam appears in his eyes—that or my imagination is running wild. "Fan'ka sounds like something you'd call a naughty child. The affectionate version would be Fannychka."

Fannychka. I like it. Fannychka Pack doesn't sound like a waist bag anymore.

Nor does Fanny Chortsky for that matter.

He narrows his eyes. "That mischievous smile… If you were thinking about calling me something like Vovochka, don't. It happens to be a character that's the butt of a lot of Russian jokes."

Huh. I had no intention of doing so, but that's interesting. And thank God he's not an actual vampire and can't read minds. "Deal," I say. "But you have to tell me one of those jokes."

He frowns. "They don't translate well."

"That's fine. I still want to hear one."

"Okay. Bear in mind that Vovochka is usually a misbehaving child. Think Dennis the Menace. Also, Russian humor can get pretty dark."

"Now I really want to hear one." I pick up my wine glass.

"Here goes: One sunny Sunday morning, Vovochka runs to his mother: 'Mom, hurry, Dad hung himself in the living room!' The mother nearly has a heart attack as she rushes to the living room—just to find it empty. 'April Fools', Mom!' Vovochka says. 'Dad's hanging in the bathroom.'"

I nearly choke on my wine.

Vlad's phone dings with a text.

He glances down, then looks at me apologetically. "The limo is outside. I have to go soon. Are you coming?"

I wipe under my nose and sneak a peek—no wine. "Is it far?"

"No, just a short drive away."

I'm about to ask more, but he loads a heaping portion of nuggets onto my plate. "Let's finish this quick. We don't have much time."

We attack the food as if we were in a hot-dog-eating contest, which doesn't prevent me from having a couple of foodgasms. Sadly, his phone begins beeping all too soon, so we leave some delicious stuff uneaten and get up.

He leaves a fortune in cash on the table and leads me to the car. As he opens the door for me, I catch a glimpse of Britney across the street. She's standing there, staring at us.

Stalker much?

Ignoring her, I climb in and sit next to where he left his laptop in hopes that he'll sit next to me.

I'm a Machiavellian genius.

Vlad takes a seat right next to me, and his lapis lazuli eyes meet mine.

My breath catches in my throat at the dark heat in

his gaze. The air in the car suddenly feels charged with so much electricity I all but smell ozone.

His eyes fall to my lips, and as if pulled by a magnet, he slowly leans toward me.

Holy Kobe Cow.

Is Vlad about to kiss me?

Chapter Eleven

*M*y heart drums a battle hymn in my chest, and my skin feels like it's burning all over. All I can see are his lips, so beautifully shaped, so soft-looking. All I can think is leaning forward and closing that small remaining distance so that—

The car rips forward, jerking us both out of the moment.

"Buckle up," Vlad says, his voice hoarse as he scoots a few inches away.

Moving like a zombie, I buckle up while he barks something at Ivan in Russian.

The car slows down.

Vlad raises the partition and turns to face me. "So, you wanted to talk."

I take in a deep breath and gather my courage. "As I said earlier, I'm doing the testing, and you can't stop me."

The amusement that touched his eyes the last time I made this ultimatum is there again. "Didn't you have someone else lined up for this testing originally? Sandra mentioned something along those lines."

I shake my head. "She flaked." There's no way I'm going into the whole succubus-turned-nun debacle with him.

He sighs. "Fine then. Test it yourself if it means so much to you."

I peer at him to make sure he's not kidding. "That's it? You're just okay with it?"

He folds his arms across his broad chest. "You'll have to convince me you can do it safely, of course."

My cheeks burn. "I can be safe. That squirrel thing was an honest mistake. Going forward, I'll do more due diligence and learn about the… err… hardware before using it. My plan is to break it all up into male and female batches, and obviously, I'll make sure to test only the female toys from now on."

He cocks his head. "Who will be testing the male batch? Or did he flake too?"

"It was the female's boyfriend, so yeah, I lost him when I lost her. My new plan is to either create an ad on Craigslist or a Tinder—"

"Absolutely not." The thunderous expression on his face must be what gave someone the idea of calling this man the Impaler.

My heart skips a beat, but at the same time, I feel my hackles rising. "No?"

The car halts.

"We're here," Vlad says through his teeth. "Do you want to wait for me in the car, or would you like to see the offices of a video game company?"

"The latter," I say, mostly to show I wasn't cowed.

In sullen silence, he holds the limo door for me, then leads me into a high-rise building, past security (where I learn he's a consultant for the video game company we're about to visit), and into the elevator.

"Look." His tone turns conciliatory as the elevator starts moving. "Getting a random guy off the street is extremely dangerous. I don't want you washing up in the New York Harbor because of this job."

He might have a point.

Before I can reply, the doors slide open and he gestures for me to come out.

"To be continued," I say and exit.

He gets us in with his ID, and I stare at the décor around us with unabashed curiosity.

The plaque on the wall is in a fun font reminiscent of comic books. It proudly states: *1000 Devils*.

That sounds vaguely familiar. I think I've played a game they made, maybe even two.

In contrast to the rather sinister company name, there are bright colors all over, and the distant laughter makes it feel like a children's playground.

This is a corporation? It almost seems like someone tried to design the exact opposite of the oppressively boring grays of our own silent-as-a-tomb office.

"First things first." Vlad leads me into a walk-in closet to the side. "Gear up."

Huh?

There are no clothes here, just Nerf guns.

Lots of Nerf guns.

Alrighty then. War it is.

Vlad grabs two rifle-shaped ones, then opens his trench coat and stuffs a handgun-shaped toy into the belt of his pants.

Lucky gun.

Shrugging, I pick out a two-handed white-and-orange blaster that reminds me of the Tommy Gun they show in old gangster movies.

"Stay back to back with me," Vlad says, no hint of a smile on his face.

I do as he says, though when our backs touch, my hormones go haywire.

I bet there's a drooling grin on my face.

We walk like that onto the main floor, like a pair of cops storming a mobster hideout.

Suddenly, an orange projectile smashes into my fake eyebrow.

"Hey!" I rub the spot before I recall that I have to be careful not to smear the drawing. "Not the face."

"Sorry," someone says.

I spot the assailant—a forty-something redheaded dude with a beer belly—and squeeze the trigger to unleash a cloud of darts into his chest.

Someone leaps out of the corner.

Vlad lunges in front of me and takes the next dart in the chest.

This time, the shooter is a lady a little older than Sandra, but I don't let that stop me from unloading the rest of my darts into her torso.

Two more attackers join the fray.

Vlad is out of darts, and so am I.

Dropping his weapons, Vlad ushers me against the wall, so that the swarm of projectiles that are meant for me smash into his back.

Wow.

He's right up against me, and it's intoxicating. I can smell the sensual notes of bergamot and citrus and feel the warmth coming off his big body.

He looks down, and our eyes meet. His pupils are dilated, his high cheekbones edged with a hint of a flush. Slowly, he bends his head and—

"Leave my brother alone," a voice booms over the sounds of the Nerf guns firing. "He's here to help."

Chapter Twelve

*B*rother?

My hormone-addled brain recalls a mention of a sibling who inspired Vlad to go into computer science.

Vlad steps away from me, rounding on the newcomer with a string of Russian.

Now that there are no delectable muscles blocking my view, I scan the speaker.

Yep. Has to be a brother. They look so alike they could pass for the same person—except the older sibling is a scruffy, laidback-looking version of the two.

"This is Fanny," Vlad says, switching back to English. "We work together at Binary Birch."

Work together—that's a nice euphemism. He could've said "works under me." No, wait, that would make me sound like a hooker.

The brother extends his hand. "Alex."

No Mr. Chortsky here, interesting. Oh, and I get the 1000 Devils reference now—Alex owns his last name, it seems.

"Nice to meet you," I say as I give his hand a professional shake.

"Step into the war room," Alex says and leads me and Vlad into a large conference room with a view of Central Park.

A bunch of people are already here, and unlike the exuberant gun-toting colleagues we left outside, they look subdued, even haggard.

"We have a problem with Squirrel Simulator," Alex says, but he makes it sound like there's a double "w" where the double "r" should be in Squirrel, and a "w" instead of "r" at the end of simulator.

Weird. He said war room without doing that, so it can't be a speech impediment.

"Again?" Vlad frowns and explains to me, "1000 Devils just released a fix for a major glitch in that game."

So, Squirrel Simulator is a game. I should've guessed that.

"Is it like Goat Simulator, but with a squirrel?" I ask.

"Much more fun." Alex's chest expands with pride. "A squirrel is smaller, so it can get into places a goat can't even dream of."

Vlad darts me a quick glance, then asks, "Did the glitch not get fixed?"

I redden. Was that glance in reference to the

"squirrel can get anywhere" comment? It might be, since in my case, a type of squirrel was up my butt—and that wasn't really fun. At least not for me.

"The last glitch is gone, but I think the big update with the fix introduced this new problem." Alex picks up a remote, and YouTube shows up on the screen in front of us.

A video starts playing with a cute squirrel scurrying under a park bench. Suddenly, the furry creature expels smoke out of its mouth, which turns it pixelated—making the squirrel look like a demon from the deepest circles of hell.

Vlad frowns. "This reminds me of that glitch in the Sims, the one that made babies look like monsters."

"It's eerie," I say, looking at the distortions in the image that look like claws and tentacles. "Almost like you did it on purpose to scare people."

"Exactly." Alex opens a laptop on the conference table and looks at his brother. "Can you check if we've been hacked?"

Vlad takes a seat in front of the laptop and starts typing away.

"Did you know cybersecurity was yet another one of my little brother's talents?" Alex asks me with a wide grin.

"Nope." I shoot a hungry glance at Vlad. Realizing the brother might catch on, I clear my throat and ask, "Have you ever been hacked before?"

"Never—and for the same reason. Vlad set up the security."

"Have you already found the bug in the code?" I ask.

"No. The development team are on it, but it's hard so far because we've been having trouble replicating the problem here in the office. The only reason I know that video isn't a hoax are the one-star reviews from angry parents whose children couldn't sleep after seeing this glitch."

"Mind if I check out the game?" I ask. "What platform is it on?"

"It's available everywhere," Alex says. "Phones, PCs, consoles—you name it."

Nodding, I pull out Precious and search the app store for Squirrel Simulator made by 1000 Devils.

I don't find it, but I do see Squiwwel Simulatow.

Alrighty then. It's *really* for kids. This explains why Alex pronounced the name that way.

I kick off a download of the game, and as I wait, I ask, "What was the glitch you just fixed?"

Wincing, Alex pulls up another YouTube video. In it, the still-super-cute version of the squirrel approaches a bully-looking kid who's holding a base-ball bat.

The squirrel halts.

The kid smashes the bat into the furry creature.

The squirrel takes flight, and flies and flies until the cityscape under him is barely visible.

Then the plummet begins.

"I take it that wasn't supposed to happen?" I ask.

"Bug in the physics engine," Alex says, sounding defensive. "We're not the first to have something like this happen. The giants in Skyrim send people flying into the sky to this day."

"Which is why we should've left it alone," Vlad chimes in, his fingers still dancing away on his keyboard.

Alex shrugs. "We were getting hundreds of bad reviews for that, not to mention the emails from upset parents."

Noticing that my download is done, I bring up the game.

Cute. I get to pick what I look like. I choose orange fur, maximum tail length, and white belly—mainly because that's how the demon squirrel from the video looked before the horrific transformation began.

The game starts with a tutorial. I learn important facts, like that my teeth never stop growing and therefore I have to gnaw on things constantly to stay healthy. It also teaches me how to zigzag when escaping dogs and other enemies, how to bury nuts so that a fellow squirrel won't steal them—sometimes even faking the burying process to mess with AI squirrel minds—and how to use my tail for balance and as a parachute during a fall or an umbrella on snowy days.

At least the realism isn't one hundred percent. I'm sure the complaining parents wouldn't like their kids to know that there's a type of squirrel that has giant genitalia—at least for a squirrel. My ex told me about them. Their shlongs are forty percent of the length of their body, and the family jewels are about half that. My ex was clearly envious, especially of the other factoid: During masturbation, these squirrels can bend over and stick their penis in their own mouth. Also, most female squirrels have multiple male partners when they're in heat—I've seen such an orgy a few times in the park.

When the tutorial is completed, I direct my furry self to scurry over to the nearby park, one that looks like the setting of the YouTube video. I figure that with my QA experience, I have as good of a chance of replicating this bug as the next corporate drone.

I climb every tree in the vicinity, eat some nuts, seeds, and a few eggs from an unattended bird nest—but look cute and cuddly throughout.

Hiding nuts doesn't help, nor does hiding inappropriate things, like the lollipop I steal from a toddler.

I'm about to give up when I spot something that strictly speaking shouldn't even be in this game—a cigarette butt under one of the benches.

I get that these are everywhere in reality, but this is a children's game.

I also recall something I read once: Squirrels are addicted to nicotine from eating leftover butts, and also caffeine from licking discarded Starbucks cups.

Would the game let me eat a cigarette butt?

Hopping over to it, I grab it in my furry paws.

Before I can put the disgusting thing in my mouth, Vlad's voice pulls me out of the game.

"It's hard to prove a negative," he says. "But as far as I can tell, you haven't been hacked."

Ignoring Alex's reply, I put the cigarette butt into my mouth as if it were a juicy acorn.

Eureka.

Instead of eating the thing, the game cuts to smoke expelling out of my mouth—which, in hindsight, was a clue—and I become demonic, just like in the video.

"I reproduced," I say.

Everyone snickers.

Vlad rolls his eyes. "Children."

"As I was trying to say, I was able to reproduce the problem." I show the screen.

Vlad stands up and comes over, invading my personal space. "How?"

Though it's difficult to think like this, I explain about the cigarette butt.

His eyebrows furrow. Then he hurries back to the seat and bangs away on the laptop again.

Alex and I watch over his shoulder.

C++ covers the screen, and Vlad mutters something as he skims the code.

"Aha," he says and minimizes the code window. He plays around in the source control repository until he has a code submission on the screen. One that, presumably, introduced the problem.

"This did it," he says, confirming my suspicion.

"Talk to Johnny Kove. If he did it intentionally—which seems to be the case—fire him."

Does he own this company also? He sure sounds like he does.

Alex looks upset. "He's one of my best developers."

"You're one of your best developers," Vlad retorts. He explains to me, "Alex originally wrote this game, as well as a few other mega hits."

"He's being too modest," Alex says. "We wrote it together, but now that he's so busy with Binary Birch projects, I work on it with my dev team."

"Well, it's your call," Vlad says, but his tone doesn't match his words. "Keep in mind, though, if the guy does something like this again, I won't come to the rescue."

Alex says something in Russian. It sounds conciliatory, but it could be my imagination.

Vlad replies sternly, and they go back and forth like that for a bit. Something tells me the topic has shifted from games to something more personal.

"Thank you both," Alex says when the sibling bickering comes to an end. "I'll walk you out."

That saves us from the Nerf gun attack. When the elevator opens, Alex glances at his brother with a mischievous expression, then faces me. "Fanny, we're having a big 1000 Devils anniversary party at my parents' restaurant next week. Could I ask you to please drag Vlad over there? It would mean the world to the family."

"You don't have to dignify that with a reply," Vlad growls.

Since Vlad ultimately pays my salary, I take that as a hint to stay silent.

The elevator doors slide shut, and Vlad jabs the button for the lobby. "Back to our earlier conversation," he says as we descend. "Did you think of a safe way to test the male batch of the hardware?"

I did, in fact, do just that. Running around as a squirrel is very conducive to plotting evil deeds, as well as testing procedures. The problem is, I don't know if I have enough proverbial balls to voice my insane idea out loud.

"Look," he says softly. "If you want to quit the project, I understand."

This again? He thinks I've chickened out? That my prudish nature has won?

I straighten my spine. "Actually, I have the perfect male in mind for the testing. Someone you'll think is safe, guaranteed."

His lips thin into an angry line. "Who?"

I take in a deep breath and call forth all of my courage. "You."

Chapter Thirteen

"*Me?*" Eyes widening, he steps back.

I'm committed now, so I barrel ahead. "It makes sense. I presume you trust yourself not to toss me into the Harbor. The privacy of the project isn't compromised. And, well"—I blush horribly—"you have the right parts for it."

Unbidden, my eyes drop to said parts, then I quickly look up.

The elevator doors open.

"Let's continue this in the car," he says, his expression turning unreadable.

Crap, crap, crap. Is he hating the idea? Hating me for even suggesting it? Ugh, how awkward is it going to be if he says no?

Am I about to get fired for coming on to my boss's boss?

We get into the limo again, sitting opposite each other this time.

He makes the partition go up. "Just to clarify: I test the male batch, acting as both giver and receiver, right? I actually already tested one of the pieces on myself after I wrote the app, so I could in theory do the same with the rest of them."

Yes! He's actually considering it. I want to jump up and down, even as the blush that had slightly receded on the walk from the elevator returns in all its glory. "That wouldn't be good end-to-end testing, and you know it. You wrote the code; that makes you biased."

His nostrils flare. "Then how?"

Even my feet are blushing at this point. "You just act as the receiver. I act as the giver, and record the testing data. It's the proper way these things are done."

His eyebrows lift. "That's stretching the definition of the word 'proper' way outside its comfort zone."

"Look." I try to mime his accent as best I can. "If you want to quit, I understand."

A slow, sensuous smile curves his lips. "I don't shy away from a challenge."

Can my panties really melt, or is that just a saying? Doing my best to play it cool, I quirk my fake eyebrow. "That's a yes, right?"

"Yes. How do you see this working, logistically?"

Holy guacamole. He's in. I got him to commit.

But what now?

On some level, I didn't expect him to actually agree to this madness, and now that he has, I'm faced with the logistics of using sex toys on my boss's boss. Logistics that will include getting him off—and recording how fast in a spreadsheet.

Or worse, recording that I *couldn't* get him off.

C++ help me, there are worse logistics than that. For example, don't most guy toys require an erect penis to go into some of the toys? How do I make sure his is ready for testing… logistically?

"You don't have to decide all this now," he says, once again seemingly reading my mind.

"Right." I clear my throat and reach for my inner QA analyst. "Off the top of my head, it would be best to use the app as close to how it was intended as possible. Meaning remotely." As in, I don't want to be next to him for the "getting the penis ready" part of these logistics.

Unless, maybe I do?

No. Must at least pretend to be professional. Or what passes for professional under the circumstances.

"Yes, doing this remotely makes sense." Is that disappointment hidden behind the indecipherable expression on his face? "When do you want to start?"

"I'm free tonight," I blurt.

Crap. That wasn't smooth. Do I look like a loser who has no life?

Recalling the scent of perfume on the testing sheet and inside the suitcase, I quickly add, "Assuming you don't have a Friday night date, that is."

He pulls out his phone and sends a few rapid-fire

texts. "My evening schedule is now cleared. This is very important."

"Why is it so important?" I ask.

What I really want to know is if it has something to do with someone who uses a little too much perfume.

He frowns. "I thought I explained this earlier. There's a chance to demo the final product to the editors of *Cosmo* in two weeks."

That's why it's important to the Belka company, but not why it's important *to him*. Oh, well. I guess he doesn't want to tell me the real reason—which might mean it has something to do with the perfumed mystery lady (or possibly gentleman—why not keep an open mind?).

If I needed another reason to keep things professional between us, here it is: Vlad might already be taken.

Who is she? the green monster of jealousy demands.

How would I know?

Find out, then tell her you humped her man with a sex toy.

Belka is probably the company she works for, so she might not care.

Plan B: kill her.

The car comes to a full stop, and with a mixture of relief and disappointment, I realize I'm home.

"So… see you tonight?" I unbuckle my seatbelt.

He exits the car and holds the door open for me.

"Unless you change your mind—which would be totally fine."

Unless I chicken out, he means.

Nope. Not happening.

Hopefully.

"Get home safe," I blurt.

Is he staring at my lips?

Am I staring at his?

A faint smile touches those lips. "You too."

"Thanks." I make a concentrated effort not to trip over something as I sprint for my door.

As I get into my building, I catch a glimpse of him still standing there by the limo, watching me.

Dashing inside my apartment, I lean with my back to the door, fanning myself.

Monkey peeks out of her little house.

"I know, right?" I say. "What did I just get myself into?"

———

After Monkey and I get our bellies full, I find creative ways to keep myself from worrying about the upcoming testing—and what works best is looking at my code.

I implement some of the easier ideas the Phantom had suggested, then check to see if he's written to me again.

He has—along with making a change in my code.

I hope you don't take offense, but I renamed all the counter variables to use the word "count," which is the Binary Birch standard. While I understand that your variation—Chocula—was a joke, it detracted gravitas from your otherwise elegant code. You can, of course, revert this change.

Huh. I, too, get the urge to change code I dislike when I see it. Especially when I spot the kind of atrocities I saw in Britney's work.

Since Phantom has a decent point there, I don't revert the change. As much as I like Count Chocula—and I go coo-coo for the stuff—the last thing I want is for the development team to think that I don't take coding seriously. For that matter, it's not good to publicize my cereal addiction so widely, especially now that I have a new delicious vampire in my life—Vlad.

Speaking of the devil, it's almost time for the testing.

As I redraw my eyebrows and in general make myself more presentable, I contemplate if the testing should take place in my bedroom or the living room. Since living room seems a tad more professional, I tidy it up, then rush to the bedroom to get the suitcase with toys. Returning, I park it next to my couch.

What should we test?

I open the suitcase, examine the male-oriented toys, and choose the one that seems the least intimidating. Still, I go on Precious and research how to use the thing—no more toy-related hospital trips, thank you very much.

The toy is a type of sleeve, and its use is usually pretty straightforward: lube it up, then stick a shlong into it. From here, the user would usually slide it up and down by hand, but the Belka model is high tech and will do the sliding up and down by itself. It'll also vibrate if that's desired.

Determined to be ready for any eventuality, I lube up mine and put a finger in.

Then two.

Interesting.

I've never put fingers inside another female—only myself—but this is eerily similar, except it feels cold. So more like a dead female, I guess.

How stretchy is this thing?

I put another finger in.

No problem.

I put in a fourth.

Still no problem.

I make a tight fist, and it slides in.

Great, I'm fisting the poor jellyfish/dead woman's vagina.

Going back to two fingers, I bring up the app with my other hand to see the options I'll need to use later.

The major buttons are "Stroke" and "Vibrate."

I click Stroke, and the sleeve tries to swallow my fingers like a hungry jellyfish.

Wow. How did they get it to move like that?

I press Vibrate next—and now it feels like that jellyfish is trying to swallow my fingers during an earthquake.

Throughout this exercise, I do my best not to think about Vlad.

Or his cock.

Or—

Precious pings with a text.

Crap. It's time.

I sprint to the kitchen, toss the sleeve into the sink, and wipe the lube from my fingers with a paper towel.

Returning to the couch, I check my phone.

Right. It's the text that will link my app with Vlad's.

As soon as I set that up, the videoconferencing part of the app comes to life.

Picking up the call, I try to be cool and not blush. This is work related. No reason to panic.

Then I see his lapis lazuli eyes gleaming behind his lenses, and all professionalism goes down the drain.

My cheeks burn as if stung by that same hungry jellyfish.

"Hi, Fanny," he says, his accent thicker than usual.

"Hi, sir." I fight the urge to salute him.

The corners of his lips twitch. "You can call me Vlad, remember?"

"Right. Vlad. I picked out the toy for today. The sleeve. It's the—"

"I know the one." He disappears from camera view, and I hear him rummaging in what I assume is his own suitcase.

When he reappears, he's holding the toy in question.

Impossibly, my blush deepens. "Yeah, that one."

"Good choice." He brushes the tip of his finger around the toy entrance—making my lady bits insanely jealous. "This is the same one I used for my own testing."

"Great." It takes effort to hold the phone steady. "So… I guess you put yourself into it?"

Echoes of my earlier logistical thoughts buzz around my head.

He needs to be hard for this. Is that my problem? Surely not.

"Do you need a minute?" I nervously lick my lips. "To watch an adult video or—"

"I'm ready." His gaze seems to be on my mouth. "Where do you want me to point the camera? I'd prefer it to be my face, but if—"

"Your face is good." The words come out like the pained croak of a toad that's been run over by an ice cream truck.

I mean I'm only human, so I really, really would like the camera pointed down, but there's no QA reason for it that I can think of, not unless I'd made the sleeve and wanted to make sure it fits snugly on his—

"I'm in," he murmurs.

Alrighty then.

That means it's my turn… to get him off.

Chapter Fourteen

*S*tay professional.
     Clinical.

Somehow.

"I'm going to test the Stroke button first," I say, and pray I don't have a stroke as I do.

He nods.

I press the Stroke button.

His pupils dilate.

An intensity dial pops up on my screen.

"I'm going to scale up the speed." Did my voice come out husky? Got to quit that.

He bites his lip and nods.

I slowly get him to fifty-percent intensity.

His jaw muscles tense and his pupils dilate even more as his eyes roam my face with the hunger of a predator.

I like it. A bit too much. I cough nervously into my fist. "Tell me if it gets to be too much."

"This is good." His breathing is clearly ragged.

Damn, this is hot.

Way, way too hot to be professional.

I never would've guessed how much I'd enjoy this. I have to constantly fight the urge to sneak my hand down so I can join him in the fun.

"I'm adding in the vibration. Okay?"

I take the grunt of his response as a yes, and click the button.

He groans, and his neck muscles tense. Then he exhales loudly, relaxing.

As I watch his O-face on my screen, I nearly have that stroke.

It's official.

I brought my boss's boss to orgasm.

Yep. That happened.

At least, I think he orgasmed.

Better check.

"Did you finish?" I ask, my voice barely above a whisper. "I need to know for the documentation."

There. That sounds semi-professional—especially if I were a courtesan.

"Yes. It was intense." His voice is raspier than usual. "When I used the same toy on myself, it felt much less so."

"Huh," is all I can say at first. "Must be like tickling yourself. I wonder if my testing earlier wasn't valid since I also did it on myself."

What am I saying? Why did I go there?

Probably because I want him to get me off more than anything in the world.

He tilts his head, eyes fixed on me intently. "If you want to retest, I can help."

"Right," I hear myself saying as if from a distance. My heart pounds in my chest. "Good idea."

What? a part of me shouts. *Are you so horny your brain has stopped working?*

"I better hang up now," he says. "Have to clean up."

Clean up. Right. Because I made him come. My face burns bright again, even as disappointment snakes through me.

I'm not ready for this to end.

"When should we resume?" I ask, trying to keep my tone even. Professional, as befits an interaction between an employee and her boss's boss. "Tomorrow?"

His eyes gleam. "I appreciate your enthusiasm, but I wouldn't want to make you work on the weekend."

Ah, right.

It's Friday night.

I forgot that—along with my name.

"Weekend is no problem," I manage to say. "I did all that resting. This isn't going to eat up my whole day anyway. We'll just do one more piece of hardware. You said this was important."

Do I sound overeager?

Am I overeager?

"How does eight p.m. tomorrow sound?" he asks. "Unless you have plans?"

So, he and the perfume lady aren't meeting on Saturday night either. That raises the chances there isn't anything going on between them—unless whatever is going on doesn't require formal dates, that is.

I take in a deep breath. "I'll clear my evening schedule."

"See you then," he says and hangs up.

I make sure he really hung up, then grab a female toy at random and finish myself off to regain a semblance of sanity.

Giddy with relief, I document today's testing, finish my daily routine, and go to sleep.

The next day goes by in a haze.

I code more of Phantom's suggestions, play with Monkey, and in general try to keep my mind off the big event that's happening at eight.

A package from UPS comes in the afternoon, filled with eyebrow paraphernalia. It takes me a while to try out the indelible eyebrow pencil, eyebrow powder, and the temporary tattoos, but the winning look turns out to be the stick-on human hair eyebrow wigs, proving once again you get what you pay for.

Doing my best not to think about where that human hair actually came from, I go about my day until I get a call from Ava.

"Have you been avoiding me?" she asks instead of a hello.

"No," I say.

She huffs. "You didn't reply to any of my texts."

"Fine, maybe. I just had a lot going on."

There's a prolonged silence on her end of the line. "Is it Impaler related?"

"Yes." I tell her what happened.

"OMG," she squeals when I'm done. "You're such a hussy. I love it!"

"Am not. We're keeping things strictly professional."

"Uh-huh. Denial is not just a river in Egypt."

I roll my eyes. "He might have someone. We work together. I—"

"For tonight's testing, choose that prostate toy," she says, and I can almost hear her grinning. "Guys can be touchy about their butts, so if he lets you shove something in there, he's into you, for sure."

My face burns like the surface of the sun. "We're testing remotely, so any shoving will be of his own doing."

"Tomato, tomahto. End result: toy in butt."

"Well, he agreed to test all the boy toys." I fight the urge to scratch my human hair stick-ons. "I assume he realized the squirrel was on that list."

"Trust me. He might not have connected the dots all the way up his rectum. If he doesn't back out when you bring this up, it means something. At the very least, serious dedication to work, but more likely proof he's really into you."

I scratch the eyebrow after all. "I guess. I don't see how it will hurt."

"It might hurt him," she says with a giggle. "Make sure to use lots of lube and take it nice and slow. When I do that sort of thing, I like to start with a little bit of—"

"TMI," I shout and begin singing Happy Birthday as loudly as I can.

"Fine," she says. "I better go check on my patient anyway."

I feel a pang of guilt. I haven't even asked her where she was. "They're having you work yet another weekend?"

"I'm used to it," she says. "Keep me in the loop. Byeee."

"Bye." I hang up.

For the rest of the day, I research every toy in the suitcase and ponder an important question: Which toy should I let him retest on me?

After a long deliberation, I settle on the clit vibrator. My own session with it was super quick, which might be good for the first time with Vlad.

First time.

There will be a second. And a third.

My heartbeat skyrockets, and I begin to hyperventilate—but then the videoconferencing part of the app comes to life, so I take in a deep breath and accept his call.

Damn. I almost forgot how hot he is, with those sculpted features and dangerously kissable lips. And that lock of hair is at it again, taunting me, making my fingers itch to touch it.

"Hi," I say, trying not to drown in his intensely blue gaze.

"How's your weekend so far?" he murmurs.

"Keeping busy," I say on autopilot. "How about you? Do something different?"

He seems to seriously consider the question—like someone who's never made small talk before. "I took Oracle to a rodent specialist," he finally says. "That doesn't happen often."

I blink at that nonsensical sentence, then grin as I decipher its meaning. "I assume Oracle is a rodent? Otherwise the specialist would be pretty confused."

He returns my smile. "Oracle is my sea piglet."

I arch a human hair stick-on. "What's a sea piglet? Not those horrific-looking sea cucumber creatures with seven legs that lurk in the ocean depths, I hope? Those are not rodents. More like miniature Love-craftian monsters."

His smile widens. "Sorry, it's the one English word I often mess up. I meant *guinea pig*. *Sea piglet* is a literal translation of the Russian term. The 'guinea' part of their name never made sense to me. The animals are from the Andes mountains of Peru, so—"

"Wait, you have a guinea pig?" I squeal the question, almost like a regular pig.

"Yeah. Why?"

"I have one also," I say proudly. "Her name is Monkey."

"Seriously?" The smile is a full-on grin now. "Show me."

"I'll show you mine if you show me yours," I say —and blush instantly as I realize how that came out.

The camera blurs as he gets up. I catch a glimpse of a room the size of my living room but filled with ramps, toys, hay, and other guinea pig goodness. In the middle of it all is a fluffy orange creature with fur that goes down to its feet.

"That's Oracle," he says. "She's a Coronet."

Huh. Now I feel like a bad piggy mom. I don't even know what variety of guinea pig Monkey is. Nor have I ever taken her to a rodent specialist. I thought a regular vet would suffice.

Hey, at least I didn't call her Oracle, which I presume is a reference to the database company.

It could've been worse.

He could've named her Microsoft.

Realizing we're at the "I show him mine" stage of the proceedings, I grab a seedless grape to lure Monkey out and point a camera at her when she starts munching on it.

"So cute," he says. "Looks like an American breed."

"Don't worry, yours is almost as cute," I say.

It's a lie. His is actually cuter, but I can't say that in front of Monkey. She'll never forgive me.

He goes back to where he was sitting earlier. "We

should organize a playdate. Oracle doesn't display any signs of loneliness, but I sometimes worry about her. And I've heard two females might get along well."

"A playdate?" I look at Monkey for feedback but don't get any. "Is Oracle sick, though? You said you took her to a specialist—"

"No, that was prophylactic. She got a clean bill of health."

Should I take Monkey to a vet prophylactically? In my defense, I don't even go for annual checkups myself.

"Monkey might enjoy a playdate," I concede. "How would that work logistically?"

His face smooths out, assuming his signature unreadable expression. "Let me look at my schedule after we're done. I'll text you the details."

After we're done.

I almost forgot what we're here to do.

My pulse picking up, I return to my place on the couch. "Back to business?"

He nods. "What's on the agenda today?"

"Umm. I've chosen the hardware but haven't decided who should go first."

His eyes gleam behind the lenses of his glasses. "How about ladies first? Or should age go before beauty?"

In his case, age doesn't stop him from having more beauty, but I keep my mouth shut. I don't want him to think I'm flirting. "I'll go first, and I'm keeping the camera on my face, like you did."

"Of course," he says. "Which toy are you about to use?"

Blushing, I rummage in the suitcase at my feet and pull out the clit vibrator.

His nostrils widen.

He totally just pictured me using that.

"Tell me when you're ready." His words sound strained.

"Give me a second." Eyes locked with his, I slide down my panties with my free hand.

Now his eyes widen.

I bet he knows what I just did outside his view.

My cheeks burn horribly, but something about the scenario is more arousing than embarrassing, which is embarrassing in itself.

Underwear off, I press the toy to my clit.

Chapter Fifteen

"*R*eady," I whisper. "But go easy with the intensity."

His finger grows big on my screen as he presses the "On" button.

The most minute vibration begins.

Wow.

I'm already on the verge.

His eyes roam my face.

The vibration intensifies.

Heat spreads through my core.

Must. Not. Moan.

The speed slows.

What the hell? The orgasm that was almost there begins to slip away.

Is he teasing me?

The speed increases again.

Then slows.

Then speeds up.

"Don't stop," my mouth says without my conscious permission.

Is that a satisfied smile? My vision blurs because the speed skyrockets.

I can't help but moan. And moan again.

The speed increases once more and takes me fully over the edge, which is when I cry out in pleasure.

Hey, at least I didn't scream out his name.

Feeling melty aftershocks, I move the toy away and try to catch my breath. "That was definitely more intense than when I was doing the driving."

"Told you," he murmurs, looking a little smug. "Now, do you want to be done for the day?"

"Nice try. Your turn now."

He arches an eyebrow—a real one, which makes me jealous. "Which toy?"

Until now, I wasn't sure if I'd do what Ava suggested, but because he played with the speeds, making me moan like a porn star, I decide to go for it. "Since we're in retesting mode, I was thinking the squirrel."

The hint of smugness disappears from his face, replaced with his usual indecipherable expression. He rummages somewhere and holds up the butt toy to the camera.

My sphincter nervously squeezes. It might have PTSD. "Yes, that." Wait, was I trying to sound sultry? "Unless you want to officially chicken out?"

"Why would I chicken out?" he asks calmly. If he minds this, he hides it well.

"No reason. Tell me when you're ready."

As he lubes up the toy, I do my best to keep a poker face.

One of his hands disappears from my view, and I fight the urge to giggle.

I can't believe he's really doing it.

He's putting—

He winces slightly. "Ready."

Does he look hesitant? Do I care?

A professional wouldn't care.

This is just testing, after all.

The familiar "P-spot stimulation" button appears on my side of the app. Feeling disproportionally naughty considering I'm just pressing my phone's screen, I launch the squirrel.

He looks thoughtful as the toy looks for his prostate.

I hold my breath.

If there's still a bug in his code, the toy might miss the prostate, and we'll have another hospital visit on our hands.

Nope.

The screen informs me that the squirrel has reached the promised land that is Vlad's prostate.

I clear my throat. "Last chance to back out."

"I'm good." The words don't match his expression, but I take them at face value and jab the "On" button.

An intensity control panel shows up. Feeling merciful, I set the vibration to its minimal level.

His eyes widen.

Is that a good sign? I've never played with this stuff before, so it's hard to tell.

Cautiously, I up the speed a smidge.

His breathing becomes ragged, and the veins on his neck pop out.

He's enjoying it, right? Did we need a safe word for this?

Figuring he'd say stop if needed, I up the speed a little bit more.

"Fanny!" he grunts.

Fanny, speed up or stop? I keep the speed the same.

He grunts again, this time clearly in pleasure, but the O-face is different today… almost as confused as it is blissed out.

I stop the vibration.

He sits there, breathing heavily.

"It happened, right?" I fight the urge to add, "Was it good for you?"

"Oh, it happened." His voice is hoarse. "It was very different, though. I've heard about orgasms without penile stimulation, but——"

He stops talking, no doubt realizing the question-able professionalism of "penile."

Blowing out a breath I didn't realize I was hold-ing, I order the squirrel to get out of him.

"You okay?" I ask when I see him wince again.

"All good," he says. "But I have to go now."

I bite my lip. "We'll get in touch tomorrow?"

"I'll text you," he says and hangs up.

I stare at the blank phone.

Well, that just happened. I violated my boss squared. Gave him a sexual experience he's never had before—a new type of orgasm, in fact.

But was his willingness to do that proof that he's into me, as Ava suggested?

Nah. I bet he just said yes because he's that dedicated to this project and/or open-minded. Which makes me wonder if he'd let me—

No. Stop that.

I get up, clean myself up, have a snack, and stumble into bed.

For the entire night, my sleep is restless and dreams are of the wet variety.

Chapter Sixteen

a text from Vlad is waiting on my phone first thing in the morning:

Sorry if the end of testing was a little abrupt last night.

Huh. I didn't even think about that. Now that he's pointed it out, it's understandable. If I were the one with a toy in my butt, I'd have hung up even faster than he did.

No problem, I reply and even add a smiley emoji.

A new text arrives instantly:

What's Monkey's schedule like? I figured I'd introduce her to Oracle today, and if they like each other, we can set up that playdate.

Introduce guinea pigs? What would it look like if they did or didn't like each other?

Given that I find the playdate idea adorable, I reply with:

Monkey is wide open today.

Wait, did I just make Monkey sound like a slut?

How does eleven sound? he asks.

I check the clock. There're a few hours left, so I agree with this too, a little more hesitantly this time. The logistics of the introductions are a little fuzzy in my head. Are we doing it over video conferencing or—

Great. Oracle and I will be over at eleven.

Over? As in, to my place? I knew something about this introduction business was dodgy.

Well, it's too late to back out of it now. Plus, a part of me loves the idea of seeing Vlad in person.

See you at eleven, I text him and launch into a cleaning frenzy.

By ten fifty-five, my place is cleaner than it's ever been, and I'm wearing my nicest casual dress, plus the premium eyebrows.

"You're about to make a friend," I tell Monkey.

The door rings.

My heart leaps into my throat. He's a little early. I sprint over to the door and open it.

Vlad is frowning on the other side. "You don't have a peep hole, yet you didn't ask who's there."

I just stare at him.

He's got his usual black trench coat on, but the blue shirt underneath is more casual than the dark, crisply starched ones he wears in the office—though not by much.

"What if I were some criminal?" The deep blue eyes are glaring at me disapprovingly, and I finally realize what he said.

"You told me you'd be over at eleven." I try not to sound defensive. "What are the chances a criminal would come to kill me at that exact time?"

"Still, I—"

"Is that Oracle?" I point at the creature in the carrier he's holding. "She's even cuter in person."

His stern expression warms as he follows my gaze. "I hope this works. It'll be fun to see her play with a peer."

"Well, come in and let's do this," I say, gesturing toward the living room.

He takes off his shoes—probably a Russian thing—then walks into the living room and over to where Monkey lurks.

As he passes by me, I detect a faint hint of that same woman's perfume I smelled earlier.

Shit. Was he with her, whoever she is?

Asking would be extremely inappropriate; we're supposed to be acting like colleagues, not jealous lovers.

Smash something, the green monster demands.

Now you sound like the Hulk.

Smash her head.

Correction, you sound like a homicidal maniac.

"Hi, Monkey," Vlad says in a tone that sounds suspiciously like baby-talk.

Monkey watches him with unusual interest.

He places his carrier next to Monkey's home and waits.

"What's happening?" I ask, putting the question of perfume out of my mind for now.

I'm not giving in to the green monster. I refuse to.

"This is so that they can see and smell each other, but not touch," he explains.

Monkey scurries closer to edge of her cage, and when she spots Oracle, she squeaks.

I'm not a huge expert, but it sounds like a happy squeak.

Oracle's reply squeak is similar, and she's also at the edge of her carrier. Their noses are now only a few inches apart.

"That's cute," I say as they begin sniffing each other—which kind of looks like an air kiss.

Suddenly, Monkey jumps into the air, the way I've seen her do when I think she's happy.

Oracle does the same.

"That's called popcorning," Vlad says, his gaze not leaving the pets. "Very positive sign—and unexpected so soon."

"Interesting. What's next?"

"Not sure. My research says to keep them separate for a while, but given this reaction, we could risk putting them together right away—assuming you're up for it.

"Let's go for it."

He takes out his phone and sends someone a text.

The green monster stirs. Did he just ping the wearer of the perfume?

A few seconds later, the doorbell rings.

"That's Ivan," Vlad says. "But do ask who it is before you open it."

"Yes, Mom," I say and hurry to the door, Vlad on my heels.

"Who is it?" I enunciate.

"Ivan," says a heavily accented voice.

"Can I open now?" I ask Vlad.

He nods. "Now it's safe."

When I open the door, Ivan is standing there with a huge aquarium in his meaty hands. The floor of the enclosure is scattered with toys, veggies, and other things Monkey would go gaga for.

"All new stuff," Vlad says, noticing my confusion.

"Why?"

He smiles. "Gives their first meeting a neutral space. Less chance someone will feel territorial."

"All right." I gesture for Ivan to come in.

The big man also takes off his shoes, then deposits the aquarium near Monkey's house. When she sees him, she bares her teeth at him, the way she always did with my ex.

"Monkey, you pig, don't be mean to Ivan," I say sternly.

"It's fine." Vlad glares at Ivan as though the big man had provoked the teeth-baring somehow. "Ivan was just leaving."

With a huff, Ivan stomps out of the apartment.

"Oracle doesn't like him either." Vlad takes his guinea pig out of the carrier and holds her to his face. "Do you, girl?"

Wow. His guinea pig rubs noses with him. Monkey never does that with me.

Vlad deposits his pet on the floor of the aquarium. "Do you mind if I put Monkey in there too?" he asks. "How does she feel about strangers?"

"She didn't bare her teeth at you," I say. "So go for it."

He gently reaches into Monkey's home. To my surprise, she leaps into his hands. Crazier still, when he raises Monkey to his face, the treacherous creature rubs noses with him too.

I feel doubly jealous. That should be me rubbing noses with him, or at least it should be me that my pet rubs noses with.

"You're a guinea pig whisperer," I mutter as he gently puts Monkey into the aquarium.

It's either that, or he does have those vampiric powers after all, the ones that allow him to make animals his bitches.

"Monkey probably just smelled Oracle on me," he says. "They're clearly soulmates."

Aww. He's right. The two pigs begin running around like a couple of happy toddlers, squealing excitedly, rubbing noses, sniffing all the toys, and eating all the veggies. Not once do they hide in the little houses available in the corners of the enclosure.

"You know, that looks like a guinea pig mating dance," I say, watching their antics. "I've seen it on YouTube. Are you certain Oracle is a girl?"

He turns my way. "Are you sure Monkey is a girl?"

I grin widely. "All I'm saying is, Monkey's not on the pill."

He feigns seriousness. "If there are piglets, I'll take them."

"If there are piglets, you'll pay child support," I deadpan.

The pigs stop the dance, plop down, and begin grooming each other.

Double aww. "Adorable."

He looks up from the pigs and scans my face, eyes gleaming. "Adorable indeed."

Chapter Seventeen

*F*or the first time since he's come over, I fully process the fact that I have him here, in my home.

He looks good here.

Like he belongs.

Wish I could keep him.

"How long should this introduction be?" My question comes out a bit breathless.

His lapis lazuli eyes capture my gaze. "The introduction is pretty much over, and is a resounding success. We're all set for a playdate. When are you and Monkey free in the near future?"

I smile. "My work schedule has been pretty chill, so any day should work."

"Speaking of work…" He steps toward me. "Are you up for more testing tonight?"

Tonight? I'm ready for some right now. The mother of all blushes adorns my cheeks as I nod.

"How about eight p.m.?"

I nod again.

He takes another step toward me. We're now close enough for me to smell his warm, sensual scent, but also that slight undertone of perfume.

He stares at my lips.

Fuck it. I'm going to ask him about the perfume.

Any second now.

Just need to make words, that's all.

The doorbell rings.

He draws back. "Are you expecting anyone?"

Still mute, I shake my head.

"Who could it be?" he asks. "Your parents? Ava?"

I force my vocal cords to function. "Ava's at the hospital. Parents have the keys to this place and, sadly, just barge right in."

He takes out his phone and sends a text.

"Could it be Ivan?" I ask.

His phone pings. "Not Ivan. Some guy. Blond, thin, with—"

I furrow the human-hair eyebrow wigs. "That sounds like my ex."

Vlad's real eyebrows snap together. "Ex-boyfriend?"

"He's been finding excuses to visit from time to time." I'm unsure why there's so much defensiveness in my voice. "A month ago, he 'realized' he forgot an Xbox game. Two months prior to that, it was a hoodie."

"He just comes unannounced like that?"

The doorbell rings again.

"Let me see if it's actually him." I head over to the door.

Vlad follows, and I feel a little giddy at the prospect of Bob seeing a guy this hot in my apartment —and reaching conclusions.

"Who is it?" I shout at the door.

"Fanny, this is Bob," the person says in the voice of the One Who Shouldn't Be Named.

I open the door.

Bob grins at me—a grin that peters out when he spots Vlad. "I was… err… in the neighborhood," he stammers. "Realized I forgot my copy of *GEB* at your house. Any chance you can give it back to me?"

I glance over my shoulder at Vlad. "*GEB* is *Gödel, Escher, Bach*."

Vlad's face is vampire cold. Maybe even liquid-nitrogen cold. "Right. The book by Douglas Hofstadter. I've read it. It's great."

That makes sense; lots of people in our industry like that book.

"You're Bob, right?" Vlad says in a voice colder than a vampire after his daily liquid-nitrogen bath.

With a noticeable gulp, Bob nods.

"I want you to think really hard about any other object you may have forgotten here," Vlad says, practically oozing menace. "This is your last chance to get it."

Was that a threat? Bob's face definitely looks like he's taken it as such.

What should I do?

"I j-just came to get t-the book," Bob says with a stutter he never had while we dated. "I can't t-think of anything else."

Vlad lays a possessive hand on my shoulder. "Fanny, do you know where the book is?"

"Sure." I make my voice breezy, mostly to cut the tension down to about-to-explode-balloon levels. "I'll go get it."

As I leave the two men behind, I wonder if there will be only Vlad by the time I get back, plus an exsanguinated husk.

Locating the book, I rush back.

Bob looks whiter than a brand-new porcelain toilet, while Vlad's eyes are like icicles as he stares my ex down.

"Here." I thrust *GEB* into Bob's noticeably shaking hands.

"Thanks," he mumbles.

"Did you think of anything else you will ever need?" Vlad's tone could cut through glass. "I mean it. This is your last chance."

"N-no. I will never come here again." The words come out as a stuttered oath. Then Bob turns on his heel and dashes away as if a thousand devils were chasing him.

It's official. My ex just got impaled by the Impaler.

"What did you say to him while I was gone?" I ask, closing the door.

"Nothing much," Vlad says calmly. "Now I've got a lunch meeting."

Before I can ask for details, he strides back into the living room, gently picks up Oracle from the aquarium, and puts her into the carrier.

"You can keep the neutral play space here," I say. "This way, it'll be ready for the play date."

Assuming the play date is still on. He looks stormy enough to cancel it.

"You sure it wouldn't be in the way?" he asks, his expression warming by a degree or two.

I wave my hand dismissively. "Leave it."

"Thanks," he says. "But it might be best to put Monkey back into her own habitat before the play date."

"I get it," I say with a chuckle. "The famous guinea pig territorialness." It's almost as bad as that of a company owner over his testing minion.

His answering smile doesn't touch his eyes.

I usher him to the door and hold Oracle's carrier as he puts his shoes back on. Handing him the carrier, I ask, "We're still on for eight, right?"

His eyes narrow. "Why not?"

"No reason," I lie. "See you then."

He heads toward Ivan's car, and I close the door, exhaling the breath that seemed to have been in my lungs from the start of the Bob debacle.

What the hell was that about? Was Vlad jealous?

No. Can't be. Bob must've inadvertently broken some Russian custom—something like "never come over unannounced." That or Vlad gets particularly hangry around lunch time.

Yeah. One of those must be it. Someone who has a perfumed sidepiece doesn't get to be jealous.

I make my way to the aquarium, pick up Monkey, and hold her near my face.

Nope. No rubbing noses for me. Clearly, that's only something she'll do with Vlad.

Figures.

I gently put the little traitor back into her home, give her a snack, and go make myself busy until eight o'clock rolls around.

Chapter Eighteen

I examine the toys I've chosen for the big testing session.

If tonight had a theme, it would be suction: The toy for him is something called a penis pump, while mine is its tiny cousin—a clit suction device.

According to my research, both of these toys are meant to work as appetizers of sorts. They draw blood to the target area, heightening sensitivity. The Belka models seem to take this a step further by incorporating vibration and who knows what else.

Since there's time, I take the pump that's a duplicate of the one Vlad will use later and stick my fingers into it.

The material is soft but not all the way jellyfish.

I turn it on.

Wow. It's like having my fingers inside a vacuum cleaner. Is this really going to feel good for him?

I turn on the vibration.

Still feels like a vacuum cleaner, just a louder one.

Turning off the pump, I take the clit sucker and slip the tip of my index finger into it before turning it on.

This feels like the device is trying to give my finger a hickey.

With vibration, it feels like it might want to keep the tip of the finger forever.

Hmm. I wonder how this will feel once it's used as directed?

Maybe I should choose a safer toy?

The videoconference feature of the app rings, and I pick up.

"Hi." Vlad smiles, his earlier grumpiness seemingly gone. "How did the rest of your day go?"

I shrug. "Caught up on some chores. How about you? Did you and Oracle get home okay?"

"I was much too busy for a Sunday," he says. "Oracle is good but acting subdued. I think she might be missing Monkey already."

Come to think of it, Monkey was a little glum after they left. Is she also missing her new piggy friend? Or maybe Vlad?

"We'll have to set up that play date soon," I say.

He nods. "You said your schedule is open, so maybe we make it a work day, sometime early in the week?"

"It's a piggy date," I say. "Now, should we get to work?"

Did those blue eyes just turn hungry behind the horn-rimmed glasses?

"Are we doing ladies first again?" he asks.

Nodding, I show him the toys I have in mind.

He unbuttons the top button on his shirt. "Let me know when you're ready."

I'm wearing a dress without any underwear, so it's a matter of a single moment to put the suction thingy next to my clit. "Ready."

His eyes darken. Has he just figured out my commando situation?

The toy comes to life and latches onto my clit like an FDA-approved leech.

Wow. The finger test didn't properly prepare me for this.

I sneak a glance under my skirt. Damn. Things are engorged. It looks as though I'm about to sprout a penis. I'm glad he can't see that situation. My heart hammers, waves of heat washing over my body as the sensations intensify.

As if from a distance, I hear him ask, "Should I up the suction?"

"No," I pant. "Let's give vibration a try."

As soon as the vibration begins, I have the most intense—borderline painful—orgasm of my life.

Something between a moan and a scream wrenched from my lips.

Then the device turns off—releasing the vacuum but also causing another orgasm.

This is when I realize that in the throngs of passion, I dropped the phone onto the couch.

Reddening to record levels, I grab it.

His face on the screen is unreadable again.

I belatedly cross my legs. "Did you see anything?"

A hint of a smile. "A gentleman never looks and tells."

That's a yes! How much did he see? And why did it all need to be red and swollen from the suction thing?

What am I saying? I'd be just as mortified if everything were nice and pink down there. Now if my old bush was still there…

Crap, I'm making this worse by staying silent. "It's your turn," I say, my brain kicking into high gear. "According to my research, you don't need to be, umm… ready for that one. The suction of the gizmo will take care of that step."

His hand disappears from view for a few moments. Then he says, "Ready."

As a testing perfectionist, I want to ask if he's starting this out fully erect or not, so I can document that fact. My mouth doesn't form those words, however, so the testing documentation will be less than perfect.

Not that it really matters. As I told him, the device makes it so he'd be hard pretty quickly—a version of the same pump is even used on ED patients.

I press the "On" button.

I can hear the motor whirling on his end of the call.

It sounds strained or something.

His eyes widen.

"I'll up the suction, okay?"

He nods.

I twiddle with the intensity controls.

He sucks in a breath.

If he wasn't hard earlier, I'd bet big money he is now—and that knowledge sends tingles into my over-sensitive lower regions.

Suddenly, there's a strange sound. Vlad grunts, but in pain rather than pleasure.

I gape at his face.

It's not his O-face. I know what that looks like now.

This looks more like an uh-oh face.

I halt the suction. "Did something happen?"

He looks down and shakes his head in disbelief. "The pump broke."

"Broke?" I look at my own version of the pump for any breakable parts and don't see anything of the sort.

"It appears to be a sizing issue." This is said almost shyly, and certainly without any hint of superiority or ego.

My eyes bug out.

A sizing issue? As in, the pump got him so big he broke the freaking thing?

How big is he?

I look at my version of the device again.

To break it, he'd need to be as large as Glurp.

Poor little pump. It couldn't take the impaling.

Shit.

Could I?

"Do you think this test was a failure?" Vlad's voice intrudes into my insane thoughts, and I realize I've been silent all this time.

I force myself to smile. "No test is a failure. We've learned something that needs to be addressed, and that's good for Belka. In this case, it's more of a hardware rather than a software problem."

He nods seriously. "You're right. I'll pass this information along to the people at Belka."

Huh. That should be a fun conversation. "How about we wrap up the testing for today?"

Because that monster cock needs to rest.

"Sure," he says. "Same time tomorrow?"

"Works for me," I say and hang up so that I can finally spring over to my utility drawer and get my measuring tape.

The pump is eight inches in length and seven in circumference.

That gives me the lower bounds of what Vlad must be packing—and it's big enough to require its own name.

I don't have to think hard to come up with one.

Dracula.

Chapter Nineteen

*M*y sleep is even more restless than the night before.

In the morning, I find an email from Sandra in my inbox. She wants to meet for an update.

I tell her I can be down at the office by 11:30 a.m.—time chosen because I, not so secretly, hope to bump into Vlad and have another lunch together.

Sandra thanks me and says that time works, so I dress in my favorite pencil skirt and blouse to look extra professional, put on my good eyebrows, and commute to the office.

As I'm about to step into our building, a classically beautiful woman catches my gaze. She's model tall, has pouty lips, shampoo-commercial jet-black hair, and striking blue eyes.

When she passes by me, I understand what's caught my attention.

It's not her looks but her scent.

I recognize it.

It's the perfume that was on Vlad the other day. It's all over her, as if she took a bath in it.

Attack, the green monster commands. *Kill first, figure out if it's her later.*

No.

I get it. Too many witnesses. Stalk her into a dark alley.

I have a meeting with Sandra.

Puny weakling.

Shut up.

Don't tell me to shut up. I'll kill you too.

A security guard looks at me suspiciously, so I get my ID out and finally enter the building.

As I step into the elevator, a guy stops the doors from closing and follows me in.

He looks familiar, but I draw a blank for a second. Then I recall that I saw him at the monthly meeting the other day. My app had decided he looks like Butt-Head; it's just harder to place him without Beavis.

"You're Fanny, right?" Butt-Head asks. "Fanny Pack?"

"That's me." I extend my hand. "And you're…"

"Mike," he says. "Mike Ventura."

I press the button for our floor. "You work in the development department, right?"

I've tested his work, so I know this to be the case, but it seems polite to ask.

"Yeah, I do," he says. "I hear you plan to join us from QA. Saw your code. Pretty elegant."

Elegant.

Phantom keeps saying that about my code.

Could Mike be Phantom? Would it be weird to just out and ask?

The elevator doors open.

He gestures for me to leave first. "If you'd like, we can get together, talk about code and whatnot."

"Sure," I say, figuring that might also be a good time to learn if he's Phantom without being late to see my manager. "Shoot me an email. It's *fpack* at Binary Birch."

There, work email.

Keeping things profesh.

"Sounds like a plan," Mike says with a wide grin. "See ya."

Waving goodbye, I sprint over to Sandra's cube.

"Things are progressing ahead of schedule," I tell her once we grab a meeting room and settle in our chairs. "Nothing to worry about."

She exhales a breath of relief. "Thank you. I'll have to give an update to Mr. Chortsky this afternoon, so this really helps."

I redden. He already knows how things are going, but I obviously can't give Sandra a heart attack by letting her know who my male tester is.

"Anything else?" I ask, eager to run to the pantry to see if he's lurking there.

She smiles. "I heard from my equivalent in the development department."

That catches my interest. "And?"

"She says they don't have an opening right now,

but that your code impressed everyone, so when they do get one, you're going to be the first person they interview." Sandra lowers her voice to a conspiratorial whisper. "The feeling I got is that the interview would be a mere formality at that point."

Yay! They like me. "Do you know how often they have openings?"

She shrugs. "Can't be more than a few months. Company's growing."

My excitement dwindles a bit. That's forever away. I should've asked for the move sooner; the countdown could've begun then.

Then again, I didn't have the app to impress everyone with.

Sandra stands up. "Thanks again. Please keep me posted on further progress."

"I will."

I wait for her to leave, then beeline for the pantry.

My heart sinks.

Vlad isn't here.

How wrong would it be if I just popped into his office?

If by "wrong" I mean "inappropriate," then very.

Daydreaming about his eyes, I pour myself some hot water. As I'm putting in the tea bag, the cup slips off the edge of the counter, the water spilling everywhere.

Crap. At least I didn't get burned.

Grabbing some napkins, I bend over and begin to dab at the liquid. My skirt makes a strange creaking noise—it might be too tight for this maneuver—and I feel it rolling up my thighs.

Crap. Is that air I'm feeling on my thong-clad—or rather, un-clad—butt?

I smell citrusy bergamot just as someone clears his throat.

I straighten so fast I nearly give my spine whiplash.

Of course.

It's Vlad.

It wasn't enough that he saw my vag last night; now he's seen my butt too.

Does he at least like it?

I discreetly check his pants to see if Dracula is showing.

Yep. There's a bulge. A nice, big one.

"My eyes are up here," Vlad says.

Oh shit. Now he's caught me staring at his crotch.

At work.

Jerking my head up, I catch my reflection in his glasses.

Surprise, surprise. My burning cheeks are redder than a rhesus monkey's butt.

Like a case of déjà vu, Britney walks into the pantry at that very moment, her eyes jumping between me and Vlad.

"Lunch?" he asks me as soon as he spots her.

I nod, toss the wet towels into the garbage, and sprint out of there as if Britney has sprouted boils.

An elevator ride and a short walk later, I find

myself in the same restaurant as the last time—except now I'm wiser and order the children's menu right off the bat.

"The kids' menu for me too," Vlad tells the waiter.

"You don't have to always get the same thing I get," I say, still flushed and flustered from the tea bag incident. "Why should you miss out on tuna eyes, or cobra heart, or whatever else the chef has decided to cook up today?"

"We do have the *sesos* tacos you like," the waiter chimes in.

My Spanish is so-so, but I'm pretty sure *sesos* is brains. Can someone say *mad cow disease*? At least I hope we're talking cow and not, say, honey badger brains.

Vlad looks intrigued by the brains. I guess vampirism has gotten tiresome, and he's ready to try being a zombie instead.

"Seriously, have the chef's choice," I say. "Otherwise I'll feel bad."

Vlad smiles. "If you're sure."

"I insist," I say and mean it. The other alternative would be for me to get the special with him, and my stomach isn't strong enough for that.

Vlad looks up at the waiter. "Since the lady insists, I'll have the chef's choice after all."

"Of course." The waiter pours us some wine and makes himself scarce.

Vlad raises his glass. "To your health."

Do I look unwell? "Same to you." I raise my wine ceremonially and take a dainty sip.

He puts down his glass.

I do the same, and get distracted by his fingers again—specifically, the urge to lick them.

"Can I ask a personal question?" he asks, snapping me out of my inappropriate reverie.

I quirk my left human-hair eyebrow wig. "Only if I can ask you two in return."

His eyes glimmer with amusement. "Traditionally, these things go quid pro quo."

"I scorn tradition," I say with mock seriousness. "One personal question for the price of two, final offer."

"But you will answer anything I ask," he says. "Truth or Dare rules apply."

"Deal," I say and can't help but feel I might regret it.

"Why did you break up with the book picker-upper?" he asks, his blue eyes narrowing like some truth detection machine.

I was right. I already regret the deal we made. "You mean Bob?"

"If that's his name," he says with noticeable distaste. "The person who couldn't just get himself a new copy of *Gödel, Escher, Bach.*"

I take a bigger sip of my wine. "I didn't break up with him. He broke up with me."

Vlad's eyes widen—which flashes me back to the

other day when he was enjoying himself under my control. "Why would he ever do that?"

The way he puts that question makes me feel warm and fuzzy inside. Except I don't want to answer that. Not even a little.

He pushes his glasses higher up his nose with one of those lickable fingers. "You want to back out of our quid pro quo?"

I lift my chin. "I already answered your question, so you owe me two answers."

"You know what I meant to ask." He picks up his water. "Do you really want to weasel out on a technicality?"

I take yet another sip of wine for bravery. "He thought I was unadventurous."

Vlad chokes on his water. "Bullshit. You? You're one of the most daring people I know."

Whoa. I gape at him. "I am?"

"I've seen you do something daring each time we've done our testing—and what is that if not adventurous?"

"I guess." I dubiously survey the nearby tables. "But I haven't tried the food here." Or asked him about the perfumed lady.

He waves his hand dismissively. "I bet you could eat it if you wanted to. But why? Food is meant to be enjoyed. If the picker-upper asked you to do something you didn't feel like doing, that doesn't make you unadventurous. His labeling you that makes him an asshole, though."

The waiter brings the food, sparing me from needing to comment on what he said.

He's not wrong, though. Bob *is* an asshole. In hindsight, I should've broken up with *him*. But I was busy with my new job at Binary Birch, and I simply didn't have the mental bandwidth to analyze my relationship. I just kind of went with the flow, even though the sex was at best meh—a situation Bob tried to fix by pushing for ever-more-exotic bedroom acts that I just didn't feel like doing with him. The final straw was after we came back from Prague, where we'd gone to the succubus show at the strip club—which I'd greatly enjoyed, by the way, due to high production values, topnotch costumes, and great acting. In any case, Bob decided that since I was down for seeing showgirls fist each other on stage, I might be cool with golden showers—and that was a hard no for me. And my hard no pissed off Bob—pun intended—who promptly broke up with me. Though sometimes it seems like he wants me back, because he keeps stopping by my place every once in a while to pick up the few items he left there.

Feeling myself getting riled up all over again—normally, I don't even like thinking of Bob's name—I focus on the food in front of me.

It's the same as last time: yuca and yam fries in bechamel sauce, bluefin tuna fish sticks, quail nuggets, and the fancy cheese quesadillas.

I don't look too much into Vlad's selection. As long as it doesn't crawl from his plate onto mine, I'm happy. In any case, my mind is still churning with unwelcome thoughts of my ex—and more annoyingly, of the mystery perfumed lady.

I really need to do something about the latter before the green monster drives me mad.

"So," I say when I finish a fish stick and a nugget. "My turn to ask a question."

Vlad slurps down something I can't—and don't want to—identify. "Shoot."

"Why did your last relationship end?" I ask, pinning him with an intent stare. "Unless… you're still in it."

Chapter Twenty

*T*here. Not very subtle, but hey.

He bites into what must be the brain-based taco, and I half expect his eyes to glaze over, zombie style.

"My last relationship was a couple of years ago," he says after he swallows. "She broke up with me because we didn't have much in common—her words, not mine."

Not enough in common? That's better than "couldn't handle Dracula."

"Since that breakup, I haven't dated much," he continues. "Not because I'm heartbroken or anything. I've just gotten very busy with my company and helping Alex with his."

So not currently dating?

Must suppress glee.

This also means the perfume lady is, at most, a

casual hookup—way better than a steady girlfriend, though still not ideal.

But, wait, is he still too busy for dating someone worthy… someone who might look like Snow White?

How obvious will it be if my second question is about that?

Transparent.

One corner of his mouth lifts in a devilish smile. "You have one more question. I'm curious to hear it."

Here's proof I'm not as daring as he thinks. Instead of asking if he's ready to date now, specifically me, I blurt, "How come there's no information about you online?"

The smile disappears. "Because I'm an extremely private person."

I heap some fries onto my plate. "That's not really an answer. *Why* are you so private?"

"Why is everyone else not *more* private?"

I grin. "Is that another question?"

He shakes his head. "Do you have any idea how many people didn't get a job at my or my brother's company based solely on the things they've posted on Facebook and Twitter? And that's a benign example. A government can do something much worse than not hire you. They can put you in jail, or place you on some list, or who knows what else. To me, the fact that millions of people share their most private moments with the world of their own free will is completely nuts. An ego trip gone horribly wrong."

"Wow. Tell me how you *really* feel," I say, mentally cataloguing what I've posted on my social media. Some of it I should probably take down posthaste.

He bites into a questionable morsel that proceeds to ooze something green and sticky. "As the saying goes: knowledge is power. I don't like giving up my power."

I reach to scratch my eyebrow, then recall its precarious nature and scratch my forehead instead. "I get what you're saying. To me, though, it sounds a little paranoid."

This time, I'm pretty sure it's a piece of blood sausage that he puts into his mouth. Hopefully made with pig's blood, but you never know.

"How about a thought experiment?" he says after the sausage is a goner. "I give you a scenario, and you tell me how it makes you feel."

"Sure." I bite into a fry.

"You met with Sandra today." This is said as a statement, not a question.

"Yeah, I did. So what?"

He leans forward. "How about if I told you that I witnessed your whole conversation through the security camera in the meeting room?"

I frown. "I'd say that was a little creepy, but hey, it's your company. Now if you said you peep into the bathrooms, that would be a different story."

"I'm not a perv." As though to contradict his statement, he sticks his fork into something fermented—

with a sticky, slimy texture that no food should ever have. "But now you're beginning to get what I'm saying. That feeling you'd have if someone did put a camera into your bathroom is what I'm talking about." Face tightening, he adds, "It's particularly developed with me, and for a good reason."

I freeze, another fry halfway to my mouth. "What do you mean? Did something happen?"

He puts down his fork. "My grandfather was executed based on a political joke a neighbor overheard."

Holy shit. I was not expecting that.

"That's terrible," I say when I find my tongue. "I'm so sorry."

"Thanks. This was before I was even born, so I'm okay."

Whew. I thought I'd stepped on a major land-mine. "That wouldn't happen here and now," I say. "What you're talking about was Soviet Russia—a totalitarian regime."

He spears another morsel from his collection— something that looks like two jumbo shrimp glued together. "You never know who'll get power and what they'll do with it."

"I guess. But you don't even have your picture on the company website. Or a bio. That's another level of caution altogether."

He devours the shrimp-looking thing so appetiz-ingly I almost want to try it too. Putting down his fork, he says, "A while back, a local paper wrote an article about my parents' restaurant. It helped the business, at first. Then, one day, racketeering mob types walked into the place, recognized my mom, and forced her to empty the safe at gunpoint. It was thanks to that article that they knew what she looked like, and that the restaurant was doing well." As he says this, his eyes get flinty, hinting at how he got his Impaler moniker.

The bite I was chewing feels stuck in my throat. I think I'm beginning to understand his obsession with privacy. If that had happened to my family, I'd be paranoid also.

"That must've been terrifying for your mom," I say, fighting the urge to put my hand over his. "Did the police catch the bastards?"

His mouth tightens. "Not exactly."

"They got away?"

"Not exactly."

I stare at him expectantly.

He sighs and sweeps his gaze over the nearby tables, as if checking for eavesdroppers. Then, in a lowered voice, he says, "Someone traced the criminals to their Russian social media accounts. Like the rest of the public, the gangsters weren't big on privacy, so they openly discussed criminal activity in their messages. The FBI got the translated transcripts of that communication through an anonymous tip. Just as the mobsters were taken into custody, their offshore bank account got mysteriously wiped out."

Whoa. Is he saying he robbed the robbers? If so,

that's pretty badass. I want to pry into it deeper, but he doesn't look inclined to elaborate. If anything, he seems like he regrets saying what he did.

Not wanting him to worry, I raise my hands theatrically. "You win. I almost feel like shutting down my Facebook and Instagram. But if I do, how will I stay up to speed on the health of everyone's cats?"

His expression warms by a few degrees, and he stabs his fork into another morsel on his plate. "You own a guinea pig. Cats are the enemy."

"True, true." I watch as he eats it with even greater gusto. Finally, I can't help myself. "Okay, I think you've inspired me to be daring and try something from the chef's selection. Assuming you don't mind sharing?"

He smiles and gestures at his spread. "Be my guest."

As I scan it all, my burst of enthusiasm begins to wane. "What would you recommend?"

"That." He points at the glued jumbo-shrimp thing. "They're divine today."

Right. That was the item he seemed to savor the most.

I narrow my eyes at the thing but draw a blank. "What is it? Or is it better if I don't know?"

He pushes the plate toward me. "It would be more daring if you *did* know and ate it anyway."

I spear one of the things with my fork. "Fine. Hit me. What is it?"

"Frog legs," he says. "French style—fried with parsley and garlic sauce."

Right. Now that he's said it, I can see it.

Not giving myself much time to deliberate, I stick the two legs dangling off the fork into my mouth.

The explosion of yummy flavor almost makes me moan in pleasure. It's like someone took the best qualities of chicken and fish and mixed them together.

He watches me intently.

"It's good," I say as soon as I can speak again. "I never exactly liked frogs, face to face that is, and wouldn't pet one, but I guess I *can* eat them."

And they're not as gross as snail eggs, that's for sure.

He nods. "I wouldn't pet a sea urchin, but they are delicious."

"Makes sense. Next time, I might just get an order of these."

"You should. Also, if you like French-inspired cuisine, you might enjoy the fare at my parents' restaurant. Speaking of…" He rubs the stubble on his chin. "Remember that party my brother invited you to?"

"The 1000 Devils' anniversary?"

"That's the one. It's tonight, and my family has been pestering me to go."

I blink. "So go. They're your family."

His gaze is intent on my face. "Would you join me? My brother did want you there, remember?"

"I think he wanted me to bring *you*, not the other way around." I sneak a worried glance at the more dubious items on his plate.

"The food will be much less exotic than here," he says, discerning my concern. "The most unusual thing on my parents' menu is probably caviar. Regular black caviar, that is—and you don't have to eat it."

Is he asking me out on a date?

No. His brother invited me first.

Still. This sounds fancy. And it's Vlad who's now pushing me to go.

His lips curve into another wicked smile. "How about we make another deal? I will go only if you go with me."

"Hey. That's not fair. That's like some weird emotional blackmail."

He cocks his head. "You're not the only one who can play hardball."

"But… tonight?" I frantically glance down at my work outfit. "I don't have anything fancy to wear."

"How about I get you something?"

"I'm not sure—"

"If you don't like the clothes, you can opt not to go."

I squeeze the bridge of my nose. "You're pushy."

His eyes gleam. "I go for what I want."

My throat suddenly feels dry, so I sip my water.

"Come on," he says. "Yes or no?"

"Maybe," I say, figuring I can always flake because

of the outfit. "Now, can we please talk about something else?"

He looks satisfied, smug even. I guess he's decided I'm going. "Well… there was an interesting computational problem today. Want to hear about it?"

Huh. Does he know about my interest in transferring to the development department? Could be. I wouldn't be surprised if he's on the same mailing list as the rest of them—and could've seen Sandra's email about my ambitions.

"Sure," I say. "What was it?"

"Have you ever heard of the Scunthorpe problem?"

I shake my head.

"Scunthorpe is the name of a town in England, and citizens of that town couldn't create accounts with AOL back in the day because the name contains the substring 'cunt,' which activated AOL's profanity filters."

I grin, which spurs him on to provide a bunch more examples of the same issue, such as when someone couldn't register a domain called *shitakemushrooms.com* because of the first four letters—never mind that the proper spelling of that particular mushroom has an extra "i" that would've fixed the problem. Or when a doctor by the last name of *Libshitz* was not able to register an email. My favorite is how the Montreal Urban Community website was blocked by web filtering software because their French name was

Communauté urbaine de Montréal, which meant their acronym and therefore website address was "cum."

"And today's problem was almost the same," Vlad says with a grin. "Our HR spam filters were blocking resumes of magna *cum* laude graduates."

As I laugh at this, his phone beeps.

"Sorry," he says after checking on it. "I have to get back to the office."

"Of course," I say.

He throws wads of cash on the table, and we hurry out of the restaurant.

"I'm going to run," he says. "See you tonight."

Before I can clarify that he *might* see me tonight, he's already crossing the street.

Crap. The clothes he gets me would have to be truly hideous for me to be able to flake without looking like an asshole. And if I do, I'll genuinely feel bad if he ditches his family as a result, even if I rationally know it would be on him, not me.

He *is* evil. But that's not news.

As I trek home, I ponder an important question: Did he invite me on a date?

We *have* been spending a lot of time together, and the testing has been hot and heavy, so I could see why he might.

But is it something I want?

Obviously, yes, at least I would if he weren't my boss squared. As is, I can't help but worry how this would look to the rest of Binary Birch. Not to mention, if we dated and broke up, would I lose my job?

Also a factor is the perfumed mystery woman. He saw her as recently as this morning—which doesn't mesh well with my fantasy of this invite being a date.

These thoughts loop in my head throughout the entire commute and when I get home. Then I start wondering when the dress is supposed to arrive and what time the party actually is.

He really didn't tell me anything.

At four p.m., my doorbell rings.

"Who's there?" I ask.

"Delivery," a distant voice says.

I open the door and see two boxes sitting on the welcome mat.

I guess that answers one of my questions.

Bringing it all inside, I open the bigger box.

There's a folded dress with a note inside:

I will pick you up at seven.

Okay, another question answered.

I unroll the dress.

It's a gorgeous little black number that might've been inspired by Audrey Hepburn's iconic look in *Breakfast at Tiffany's*.

It looks suspiciously close to my size.

I put it on.

The thing fits me down to a millimeter. Almost as if someone took a cast of my body and designed the dress around it.

Did Vlad hack some online purchase I made? Or

did he look at me so closely that he could guess my measurements this precisely?

Befuddled, I open the second box.

A pair of shoegasmic Christian Louboutin pumps is inside—and they fit me as perfectly as the dress.

What is happening?

I check myself out in the mirror and can't help but wolf-whistle.

It's official. There's no way I could say this isn't a great outfit without sounding like a dirty liar.

Taking a selfie, I text it to Ava.

The reply is instant:

Hot! What's the occasion?

When I tell her it's to go to a Russian restaurant with Vlad, Precious rings right away.

"Tell me everything," Ava demands as soon as I pick up.

I bring her up to speed, concluding with my doubts about this being a date.

"Oh, it's a date. The guy is majorly into you. He used the squirrel toy, for fuck's sake."

I squeeze the phone harder. "What about the other woman?"

"Ask him about her," she says. "Maybe ply him with a few drinks first."

"I guess…"

"No guessing needed. Do it. Also, have you done your makeup and hair yet?"

"No." I look at myself in the mirror. "My makeup isn't bad. I just got back from work."

"I'm hanging up, and you're dolling yourself up. Do you want me to send you some useful YouTube videos?"

I roll my eyes, though she can't see it. "I can use the internet all on my own. Bye."

I dive into my makeover and end up with an updo and enough makeup to make a naked mole rat look presentable. I even trim the eyebrow wigs a little and gel them up to keep the bushiness under control.

Just as I'm finishing up, the doorbell rings.

Crap. He's here.

Diving into the shoes, I click-clack over to the door.

"Who's there?" I say pointedly, so I don't get chastised for opening the door for criminals with impeccable timing.

"Vlad," he says.

I open the door.

Oh my.

Dressed in a bespoke black suit that hugs his every muscle, a crisply starched white shirt, and a black tie, he's a sight to behold.

"You look amazing," he murmurs, his eyes greedily scanning me from head to toe.

Ignoring the heat in my cheeks and other regions, I twirl coquettishly. "It's the dress you got me."

His voice roughens. "No. It's you." Before I can respond, he gestures at the limo. "Come, we're already late."

Drunk on his words, I get to the limo on autopilot.

He holds the door open for me.

With a goofy grin, I slide inside and sit by his trusty laptop—the last time, this had made it so he'd sit next to me.

Yep. He slides over, his presence making me tingly and giddy.

"Is it hot in here?" He plays with the air conditioning controls.

So hot. So take off all your clothes… "I'm okay," I lie, the words of the song playing through my head.

He gives me a warm smile and tells Ivan, "*Poyehali.*" He then raises the partition.

The car torpedoes forward, and we sit there, staring into each other's eyes like a couple of staring-contest champions.

"What's the name of the restaurant?" I force myself to ask.

His lips twitch. "On Yelp, it's listed as the New Hut."

"Any relation to Pizza Hut or Jabba the Hut?"

"The latter has two Ts in his name," he says with a smile.

I fight the urge to grab him by the tie and lick that smile. "Well, the word 'hut' doesn't make it sound as fancy as I imagined."

He adjusts his glasses. "It's fancy. The hut bit is a left-over from its longer name—The Hut on Hen's Legs."

I blink, taken aback. "That's a horrible name—no offense."

"I don't disagree. It's a reference to Russian fairy tales. A hut like that was the home of the infamous Baba Yaga. If you've seen the John Wick movies, he was for some reason compared to her constantly."

I lift a well-groomed eyebrow wig. "I've heard of her. She's a cannibalistic witch, right? Ate little children. Great association for a restaurant."

He grins. "That's what I told my parents too. They kept the name anyway. At least everyone's switched to calling it the New Hut, so less cannibalism associations."

"But why is it new?"

"Because the old one burned down, and my parents got the empty space on the cheap. They kept the name because it already had some recognition among the Brighton Beach community."

The limo comes to a full stop, and I spot a green street sign that informs me we're already on the famed Brighton Beach Avenue—or Little Odessa, as it's sometimes called.

Just to confirm this, a train makes thunderous noises on the aboveground subway tracks nearby.

Getting out, I smile at the storefronts with names written in Cyrillic and at people who look like extras in a movie about Soviet Russia.

Vlad leads me to what must be the restaurant—a giant, multi-story wooden hut with, not surprisingly, chicken legs where most other buildings would have columns.

As we walk up the creaky wooden stairs, I brush my fingers along one of the "legs."

It feels as though it's made from real chicken skin.

Raw chicken, that is.

A nice touch. Always have people think *salmonella* before a dining experience.

Inside, the place couldn't look more different from its rustic external vibe if it tried. Marble and crystal are everywhere, evoking Grand Central station and the Metropolitan Opera at the same time.

The party is in full swing, with people shaking booties on a huge dance floor.

There's also a full-on stage here, with a pudgy bearded dude wearing an outfit that shines brighter than a disco ball. In his hairy sausage-like fingers, he's holding a microphone and singing his lungs out.

So, this place isn't just a restaurant. It's also a club and a theater, it seems.

The music is played on a keyboard and sounds vaguely familiar, but it takes me a moment to parse what the bearded guy is actually singing; his thick Russian accent and this context throws me off.

The song is *Single Ladies (Put a Ring on It)*.

Seriously? Beyoncé would die laughing if she heard this butchery of an interpretation.

Vlad leans in, his breath warm on my ear. "They do a lot of covers at this place. With the American audience, expect a lot of this."

I try to ignore the pleasurable goosebumps spreading down my arm. "Can't wait."

As we proceed further, I notice that most of the patrons are software engineer types—clearly 1000 Devils' staff.

"There." Vlad touches my shoulder and points at a table to the side of the dance floor. "Come meet my family."

Chapter Twenty-One

I recognize Alex right away and guess that the older couple sitting at the table must be the parents.

The mother's makeup makes me think of burlesque dancers and drag queens, and her exposed cleavage is so big it probably has a name. Helga, maybe? She's wearing a skintight purple cocktail dress with a confidence I hope to emulate when I'm her age.

The father sports a heavy mustache and in general resembles the singer on stage—hairy and pudgy but with a unibrow that the singer must've plucked.

I again feel a slight stab of eyebrow envy. I'll never take forehead facial hair for granted again.

Neither of the parents have many features in common with the two brothers, but they both remind me of someone. I just can't say who.

"Mom, Dad, this is the woman I was telling you about," Alex says as we approach. "She saved my company the other day, and, as I hoped, has dragged Vlad over here today."

Each of the parents gives me a grateful nod.

"Oh, I can't take the credit." I smile nervously. "Vlad had to convince me, not the other way around, trust me. Nice to meet you both."

Another set of approving nods. If my goal is to get these people to like me, Alex has clearly given me a head start.

"Mother, Father, this is Fanny," Vlad says, his expression surprisingly cool.

They both get up. She's ridiculously tall—a good head taller than her husband. Must be where the brothers got their height from.

"Nice to meet you, Mr. and Mrs. Chortsky," I say, extending my hand.

The father ignores my hand in favor of giving me a scratchy kiss on the cheek.

The wife smacks him on the back. "She's an American. They don't kiss strangers, you old pervert."

"Call me Boris." The father grins so widely the edges of his mustache touch his temples.

The mother smacks his back again, then shakes my hand with a genuine smile and drags me closer. Thankfully, her kiss is of the air variety. "Forgive my bear husband, dear," she whispers conspiratorially. "Call me Natasha."

As I pull back, I do my best to keep a poker face.

Boris and Natasha? That's exactly who they remind me of—the two villains from that old cartoon show with the moose and the squirrel. They even share their names.

I bet if I used my app on them, it would confirm this too. Even their heavy Russian accents are nearly identical.

"Please, sit." Boris pulls out a chair for me—and gets another smack from his wife for his troubles.

"Thanks." I sit down, and Vlad sits next to me.

The table is teeming with plates covered by cloth napkins. No one has begun eating yet, it seems.

"Service the lady," Natasha says to Vlad sternly, gesturing at the covered food.

Service me? Maybe if he got under the table or something, but even then, it would be hella awkward.

Vlad's face is stormy as he gazes at his mother. "Shouldn't we wait for *everyone* to gather first?"

This isn't everyone?

Natasha scoffs. "Latecomers do not get to eat."

"Or drink." Boris grabs a giant bottle of Stoli and pours me a shot without asking if I want one.

He then does the same for Vlad, Alex, and his wife. For himself, he pours the vodka into a wine glass.

Natasha stares daggers at Boris. "You will have shots, like a normal person."

Boris waves for a waiter to come over and says something to him in Russian.

The waiter sprints away and returns with a

handful of shot glasses that he pours Boris's vodka into.

"How about a compromise?" Boris says to Vlad and uncovers one plate. "We'll have some pickles and a drink for now, as an appetizer."

"Whatever," Vlad mutters, then spears a pickle and deposits it on my plate.

Boris puts a pickle on his wife's plate, then his own, and Alex "services" himself.

"I claim the first toast." Natasha raises her shot glass and looks around as if daring anyone to contradict her.

Did Vlad just roll his eyes?

Natasha doesn't seem to notice. Looking at me, she says, "Only alcoholics drink by themselves, without a cause, and without a toast."

Wise. I'm not sure any of that is part of the twelve-step program, but I keep my mouth shut, opting to drink some water instead.

"As a woman in her middle years, I can be forgiven if I think about my family legacy," Natasha continues, for some reason narrowing her eyes at Alex before looking approvingly at Vlad.

Looking directly at me, Natasha raises her glass even higher. "To the health of my unborn grandchildren."

I choke on my water and begin coughing.

Boris leaps out of his chair and smacks me five times on the back.

The water comes out of my nose, and eventually, I resume breathing.

"Sorry about that," I say when I can speak. "Didn't mean to mess up your toast."

"It's fine, dear." Natasha sounds comically magnanimous. "I wasn't finished anyway."

"Go on, pookie," Boris says, greedily eyeing his shot glasses.

She nods solemnly. "May my unborn grandchildren be wealthy and joyous. May their mother stay the color of spring and roses. A source of sweet dreams to the man in her life. His attraction and inspiration. May she stay simple yet regal. A princess. The muse to an opera of love. May her days last forever and beyond. To this, we shall drink until we see the bottom of our glasses."

Amen? I feel like someone should give me an Oscar for keeping a straight face.

With a theatrical gesture, Natasha downs her shot in one gulp, then sniffs her pickle before violently biting into it.

Vlad and Alex follow their mother's example, while Boris downs one shot, then another, then a third, then a fourth, and so on until they're all empty.

Not being suicidal, I take the smallest sip from mine that I can.

Fire explodes in my mouth, then spreads through my chest and into my stomach.

Gasping, I try sniffing the pickle like everyone else did.

Nope. That makes it worse.

I bite into it.

Okay, so now I have a salty taste in my mouth on top of the burn.

"So, Fannychka, do you have any Russian in you?" Natasha asks.

If I say no, will she say "do you want some?" and point at Vlad?

After that toast, it wouldn't surprise me.

"I have no clue." I cautiously put down the pickle I was still clutching. "My parents call themselves pure-bred American mutts. I've been planning to take a DNA ancestry test, but haven't yet. But you never know."

My answer seems to please her. At least she looks approvingly at me, then at Vlad.

Boris refills everyone's shot glasses, including the half dozen of his. When he sees that mine is almost full, he frowns but doesn't say anything.

Instead, he dramatically rises to his feet and raises a glass. "The time between the first drink and the second ought to be short."

"Shouldn't we eat something more substantial than a pickle first?" Natasha hisses.

Before her husband can answer, a familiar scent reaches my nostrils.

Perfume.

The perfume.

I glance behind me.

Yep.

The modelesque woman I saw by our work building is striding toward our table on five-inch heels. Her makeup looks like war paint—perhaps due to the furious expression on her face.

What the fuck?

Did Vlad invite his side piece to a family event?

.

Chapter Twenty-Two

"*A*h, if it isn't the fashionably late," Natasha says snidely to the woman.

She was also expecting her?

"Parents." The newcomer's voice is icy. "Bros." The voice is a tiny bit warmer now. "Couldn't wait even a minute, huh?"

Bros?

Whew.

She's Vlad's sister, not his lover.

Unless there's some *Game of Thrones* crap going on, which I doubt.

Vlad stands up and pulls out a chair for her. "I tried to make them wait."

As she sits, I sneak a glance. Now that I know she's Vlad's sibling, I can see the resemblance: the jet-black hair, the blue eyes, and even the ability to put on that chilly expression.

"Bella, meet Fanny." Alex sounds placating. "Vlad's friend."

The ice queen expression melts as the heavily mascaraed blue eyes swing toward me. "Oh, you're Fanny? Nice to put a face to a name."

Face to a name? She's heard about me?

I guess Vlad could've mentioned me when she came to see him this morning. Or Sunday—he did come over smelling like her.

I give her my warmest grin. "Nice to meet you, Bella. You look amazing."

Her return smile is radiant. "You don't need to flatter me. I'm already your biggest fan. Your help on—"

"No business at the table," Vlad says sternly.

Business?

Hold up. What help does she mean? Surely not the testing we—

"Your brother is so right," Natasha says, wrinkling her nose. "No reason to talk about your work in polite company."

Huh? Is she a prostitute or something?

Vlad gives his mother a slitted stare. "Bella's company is the best in its field. They're about to get a writeup in *Cosmopolitan* magazine."

I blink a few times.

Her company.

The *Cosmo* writeup.

She owns Belka?

196

If so, I was right a moment ago. She was about to compliment me on my help with the testing.

As in, Vlad told his sister about what we've been doing.

I nearly choke again. The snafu with the pump—he was going to tell the folks at Belka they need to get more generous with sizing.

That must've been a fun thing to tell his *sister*.

"Bella shames the family." Boris's usually warm demeanor is gone.

"Bullshit." Bella glares at her father. "*You* shame the family, with your drinking and—"

"Belka, stop it," Natasha hisses. "We have a guest."

Oh, boy. Sucks to be in the middle of a family squabble.

At least I've learned something. Besides meaning "squirrel," *Belka* also appears to be the diminutive of *Bella*.

"Can we eat now?" Alex asks, and before anyone answers, he removes the cover from the plate nearest him.

"Good idea." Vlad does the same to another plate.

"I'm starving," I lie and join them in uncovering the food.

The parents and sister join us more reluctantly. They still look upset. I make a mental note to steer the conversation somewhere safe if I get the chance.

For now, I examine the food.

Vlad didn't lie. It's less weird than the chef's choice from the restaurant—not that the bar was set all that high.

"Is that a Jell-O made out of meat?" I point at the item standing next to Vlad.

Natasha smiles patronizingly. "That's *holodetz*. Try some with *gorchitza* and *hren*."

"She means *mustard* and *horseradish sauce*." Vlad puts some of the holo-whatever on my plate and garnishes it with the two items. "Try it."

I do it gingerly.

The thing tastes like a really meaty chicken soup but has that jelly texture, which somehow works.

"Yum," I tell the expectant Chortskys, and as a reward (or maybe punishment), they begin educating me about the rest of the dishes.

The main thing I learn: Russians like to pickle things I wouldn't even dream of pickling, such as watermelon, apples, grapes, and herring.

Also, there are at least four more shots of vodka and long toasts throughout the lesson. Not wanting to get too drunk, I keep sipping on my one shot glass.

My favorite dish turns out to be Oliver or something that sounds like it—I mentally call it "the kitchen sink salad." It has chopped potatoes, meat, carrots, pickles, eggs, green peas, and enough mayo to keep Hellmann's in business for a month.

"She doesn't want caviar," Vlad says when his father tries to put a crêpe and some black stuff on my plate.

I smile sheepishly. "I only dislike snail eggs and cricket flour blinis. If this is buckwheat and sturgeon roe, I'll try some."

Boris laughs. "I can't believe they made my joke suggestion at that restaurant."

"It was pretty good, actually," Vlad says with a grin.

I try the famous delicacy and enjoy it.

"That's nothing as exotic as what we had in Ecuador." Natasha looks at Vlad challengingly. "Did I tell you about *cuy asado*?"

"Fanny won't like that story," Vlad says sternly. Touching my hand, he explains, "*Cuy asado* is grilled guinea pig. Mother likes to tell that story because she doesn't like Oracle."

What? That's horrible. Monkey shall never hear of this dish—she already acts like I might eat her.

Natasha wrinkles her nose. "A rat is a rat."

Wow. So many minefields with this family.

Deciding to save the day, I ask, "Can you tell me some Vovochka jokes?"

The parents exchange an approving glance. It must look like I'm more versed in the Russian culture than I actually am.

"I'll start." Boris puts down his shish kebab. "In biology class, the teacher draws a cucumber on the blackboard and asks, 'Can someone tell me what this is?' Vovochka raises his hand. 'It's a cock.' The teacher storms off. The principal rushes into the classroom. 'Who upset the teacher, and more importantly, who the hell drew that cock on the blackboard?'"

Chuckles all around.

"I know one too," Natasha says. "The teacher says, 'Vovochka, I hope I don't catch you cheating off your neighbor on the next test. 'I hope so too,' Vovochka replies."

More chuckles.

"My turn," Bella says. "Vovochka says to his Mom, 'Where do babies comes from?' Without hesitation, she says, 'The stork brings them.' 'I know it's the stork,' Vovochka replies. 'But who fucks the stork?'"

Even though his joke was also dirty, Boris gives Bella a disapproving glare.

"Can I go?" Alex asks, and before anyone replies, he says, "Vovochka puts on rubber boots. 'Vovochka, there's no dirt outside,' his mom says. 'Don't worry, Mom, I'll find it,' Vovochka replies.'"

Again chuckles.

"That one sounds just like Vlad when he was little," Natasha says to me conspiratorially.

"That's true," Bella says with a grin.

Vlad elbows his brother. "This one wasn't much better."

"We should have another drink before the show starts," Boris says and pours everyone another round.

The show? Is that what the stage is for?

Everyone downs their vodka. Upon seeing how easily Bella does it, I knock back a full shot glass.

It must be the function of the buzz I have going

already, but the vodka doesn't burn as badly going down as it did before.

The lights dim.

What I presume to be Russian music begins to play, though to me it sounds a lot like K-Pop.

A bunch of scantily clad girls run out onto the stage. They're wearing masks from that pre-orgy scene in *Eyes Wide Shut*, but their dancing reminds me more of The Rockettes.

After they raise their legs for the umpteenth time, the masked dancers depart, and the music changes to that of *Swan Lake*.

A ballerina steps onto the stage.

At least, she's a ballerina on the bottom. On the top, she's wearing horrible makeup that makes her look like a witch—with wrinkles on her forehead so large they're sprouting their own wrinkles.

Must be a Baba Yaga impersonation. Didn't know the old witch was a dancer.

The one on stage sure is. She performs some truly acrobatic ballet moves—that is, until the pudgy singer from earlier rushes onto the stage, dressed like a child.

Yep.

That's Baba Yaga, for sure. Why else would she pantomime eating the dude?

When she's done pretending to eat him, the bearded child grabs the mic, and the music changes again.

"My milkshake brings all the boys to the yard," he sings with a thick Russian accent.

The Rockettes ladies rush back, also wearing Baba Yaga makeup. Each of them holds a toy that reminds me of the killer Chucky doll—and these dolls are missing random limbs.

Did the Baba Yagas get peckish off stage?

Instead of kicking up their legs like before, the Rockettes/Baba Yagas launch into the famous Russian Cossack dance—the one with lots of squats and leg thrusts.

For elderly witches, they're incredibly athletic.

From here, the show gets even weirder. There are Cirque du Soleil-style acrobats dressed like Teletubbies, jugglers pretending to be bears, a clown straight out of Stephen King's worst nightmares, and a Baba Yaga on a unicycle for the finale.

When it's done, everyone begins to clap, and I join in.

"Ladies and Germs," the singer dude says after the ovation, sweat beading on his brow. "I want to see you on the dance floor." And just like that, he starts butchering Madonna's *Like a Virgin.*

"What did you think of the show?" Natasha asks me, beaming with pride.

Did she choreograph it? "It was... very interesting."

"I am glad to hear it," she says. "We had to simplify it for the American audience."

Simplify? The original must've been the equivalent of an LSD overdose.

"Ask the lady to dance." Bella gives Vlad an exasperated glare. "You're making the family look bad."

"Yeah, bro," Alex says. "Dance."

Smiling with his eyes, Vlad stands up and extends a hand to me, Prince Charming style. "May I have this dance?"

I leap to my feet before my brain can even think about vetoing this questionable idea.

With a knowing smirk, Bella rushes to the stage and yells something to the singer dude in Russian.

He nods.

The music changes once more to a slower song I don't recognize.

Vlad takes my hands like a professional ballroom dancer.

Heat spreads through my whole body from his touch—as though I have vodka for blood.

He pulls me closer.

I swallow my heart back into my chest.

We start to slowly sway to the music.

Can you have a heart attack from being too turned on?

"Bésame," the pudgy dude sings, and for the first time, I feel like he's in his element. "Bésame mucho."

Why, oh why, did I ever learn Spanish? That's "kiss me a lot"—which is exactly what I want Vlad to do to me.

Around us, some of the 1000 Devils' staff get the same idea. People are making out left and right. Hopefully, they're each other's significant others, and not, like in our case, bosses and their subordinates once removed.

Vlad leans down.

I shouldn't kiss him.

But I really want to.

But I mustn't.

He locks eyes with me.

Not fair. It's harder to control myself when looking into those hypnotic blue depths.

And what if he kisses me?

I think he might. And if he does, I won't be able to resist. I'm only human.

He pulls me even closer, and our lower bodies touch.

Holy phallic symbols.

Is that the proverbial flashlight in his pocket, or is Dracula very happy to see me?

I should step back, but I can't.

My legs refuse to move away—not even when Vlad slowly lowers his head, as if his mouth is drawn to mine by a puppeteer's string.

Got to do something. Now.

"We should test today," I blurt, stopping him an inch from my lips.

Eyes gleaming, he lifts his head. "Should we?"

"At your place." Wait, what? How is that better than kissing? This is clearly the hormones and the vodka talking.

His nostrils flare. "Now?"

"It *is* a school night." School night? Did that pop

into my head because this is so much like the fantasy of a prom I never had?

"Let's go." He guides me through the slow-dancing throngs of software engineers.

Before I can blink, we're in the limo again.

"What about your family?" I say as Ivan floors the gas pedal.

Vlad takes out his phone and sends a few rapid-fire texts.

A bunch of replies arrive immediately.

He rolls his eyes. "To sum up, everyone liked you. A lot."

Why do I have the feeling the actual texts mentioned unborn grandchildren or worse?

"Good to know." The words come out too breath-less for my liking.

"First things first." He reaches into a drawer on the side and takes out something resembling an asthma inhaler. Changing the mouth piece, he thrusts the gizmo in my face. "Blow."

My cheeks burn. Apparently, they pictured my lips around Dracula's shaft, not this device.

"What is that?" I ask, though I can guess.

"A breathalyzer. I want to make sure you're not intoxicated."

Huh, okay. Shrugging, I blow into the thing. I took a drug test before I started working for Binary Birch; this is not that different, I guess.

He frowns. "Point-zero-five percent. I think we're going to take you home."

Is he calling me a lightweight? I lift my chin. "Below eight is safe to drive in NYC."

His frown deepens. "Do you have a car?"

"No."

"Good. Don't even think about driving in this condition."

If the idea was to ruin my buzz, he's definitely succeeding. "Why do you have a breathalyzer here?"

He nods at the driver's section. "I do random checks, especially around the holidays. Russians make fun of drink-and-drive regulations. Ivan isn't allowed to have any alcohol when on duty."

Suddenly feeling mischievous, I lick my lips as seductively as I can. "You sure you want to take me home? The testing is oh-so important."

His jaw flexes. "Fine. Let's go to my place. I better keep an eye on you."

Wow.

His place.

This is really happening.

I sober up some more. Suddenly feeling shy, I voice something that bothered me in the restaurant. "Do you not get along with your parents?"

He shakes his head. "When I visit them one-on-one or with Alex, we get along just fine. I just don't like bigger gatherings because of how they treat Bella. She's a great sister and an amazing daughter—not to mention, an MIT grad—but they don't appreciate her."

I frown. "Because of her sex toy company?"

"No. It started much earlier. Bella was a tomboy as a kid, which our mother hated. In general, Bella has always been a free spirit, and I guess my folks didn't like it that she didn't fit the mold they had in mind for her. They always think the worst of her. Like they claim she does drugs—but she doesn't. They think she's promiscuous—but she isn't. It's infuriating."

"That sucks." I cover his hand with mine. "I know about not meeting parents' expectations. And the funny thing is, I think mine would love to swap me for Bella."

His expression warms. "Well, at least mine love you."

"Because they think I'm a prude goodie two shoes?" The question comes out more bitter than I hoped.

He leans in, the corners of his mouth tilting up. "If only they knew what you wanted to do at my place."

Even my blush blushes. "Too bad that's cancelled."

He pockets the breathalyzer. "Maybe not. Depends on your liver function."

Oh?

The car stops, and before I can respond, he opens the door for me.

His building is modern and pricey-looking. He waves at the security guy as he leads me to the elevator and presses the button for the penthouse.

Is this really happening?

I will my body to detox the alcohol as fast as it can.

The elevator opens into a large hallway.

Vlad holds the doors for me. "Welcome to my home."

I stumble out of the elevator.

This is surreal.

I've willingly come to the Impaler's lair.

Chapter Twenty-Three

"**K**itchen is through this corridor." He leads the way.

As we walk, I gawk at everything.

The place is huge, especially for New York. The décor reminds me of our office—cold, modern, spotless. But unlike at work, there are human touches here as well. Specifically, posters of *The Matrix* movie franchise. And I mean a lot of posters. In multiple languages. Of every character. There are even posters tangentially related to it, like the one that states, "In Soviet Russia, Bullet Dodges You."

We enter the kitchen.

"Sit." He presses a button on an espresso machine. "Milk, sugar?"

"Just black is fine." I plop on a chrome barstool. "So, let me guess. *The Matrix* is your favorite movie."

He cocks his head. "What gave me away? Was it the trench coat?"

I want to smack myself on the forehead. He loves that movie so much he even dresses like the characters.

How did I not pick up on that?

I grin. "Oracle. That's also a reference, isn't it?"

He pours two cups of coffee and puts one in front of me. "Tell me you like the first *Matrix*."

"I don't like it." I blow on my coffee. "I love it. I've been Trinity for every Halloween since I've seen it."

He gives me such an admiring look that, for the first time ever, I wonder if this could actually work between us.

Whatever *this* is.

We love the same movie.

We're into coding.

I find him attractive, and he clearly doesn't think me hideous.

If only I'd met him outside of work.

"Every programmer likes *The Matrix*, at least a little," he says. "How can we not? The hero is one of us."

I take a big sip. The coffee is good, smooth and only moderately bitter. "How psyched are you about the fourth one?"

He grins. "Since they confirmed its existence a few months back, I've been counting down the days."

Hmm. I wonder if he'd take me to the premiere.

"What's your favorite scene?" I ask.

He tells me, and I share what mine were. Then

we talk about other movies we like, and here, too, our likes and dislikes fit together like pieces of a puzzle.

"Can I see Oracle's room?" I ask when the coffee is gone.

With a wide grin, he leads me there.

It's as big as it seemed on the screen. There are millions of people in NYC who have less square footage than this lucky pig.

"How are you feeling?" he asks. "Still drunk?"

This again? I glare up at him. "I wasn't drunk before. Even less so now."

He pulls out the breathalyzer. "If you're below point-zero-four, I'll clear you for testing."

Testing. Crap. I totally forgot about that. Do I want my alcohol to be low or high?

I blow into the gizmo.

"Good enough," he says. "We can test—if you're still up for it, that is."

My cheeks turn redder than the Soviet flag. Can I back out of the testing now, after dragging us from the party under this pretext?

He might've been right earlier. I was drunk. How else to explain that bold invite?

I take a step back, frantically trying to think of ways to minimize the insanity of what's about to happen. "We keep things professional."

He steps toward me. "I wouldn't have it any other way."

"I'll use the Kegel balls. This way, I keep my

clothes on." I feel like I just might fall through the floor as I say it.

He loosens his tie. "Is there a guy equivalent to those balls?"

"No. I mean, there's the cock ring, but I imagine Dracula won't fit inside your pants if—"

He lifts an eyebrow. "Dracula?"

I didn't think I could redden more, but here we go.

Oh, well. Might as well fess up.

"I often nickname things." I glance down at my chest. "I dubbed the girls Pinky and the Brain, if that makes your ego feel any better."

He stares at Pinky and the Brain for a second too long, then raises his gaze back to my face. "You don't look at Dracula, and I don't look at you when you're using the balls." He takes off his glasses and puts them on a nearby table. "This way, I can't see much anyway."

I suppress a semi-hysterical giggle brought on by the phrase "using the balls." "Where do we do this?" I ask.

"Follow me." He leads me into his giant living room. "There." He points at a twin of my suitcase. "Get what we need."

I fish out the toys in question and hand him the cock ring, my face burning the entire time.

Must. Not. Think what Dracula would look like with that bling on.

As he takes the ring, our fingers brush, sending shivers down my body.

Perfect. Now I won't need any lube for the Kegel balls.

"Where's your bathroom?" Did that sound husky?

He points at a nearby door.

I lock myself in, take off my panties, and wash my hands and balls. The Kegel balls, that is. Thus far, no matter how ballsy I feel, I've never sprouted a pair, thank uterus.

Just in case, I lube up the balls and gently slide the first of the pair in, then the string that holds them together.

Feels pretty neutral so far.

Making sure to leave the removal loop out, I let the second ball join the first, and push them in as far as I'm comfortable with.

Hmm. This way, they feel tingly, and it's not a big effort to keep them in.

I could probably walk around like this all day—which, of course, would be a bad idea. Vlad could then activate the vibration at any time, even if I'm at the DMV or the fish market, or at a meeting with Sandra.

I pace from sink to tub.

Yep.

Thanks to my pelvic floor muscles, the balls stay put.

Still, walking like this is a little scary. This must be

what it's like for guys to walk around worrying about their balls all the time.

I come back to the living room and find that he's dimmed the lights.

Is this to lower visibility or to set a sexy mood?

He darts a glance at my skirt, then quickly drags his gaze to my face. "All good?"

Is that hunger in his eyes? I squeeze my muscles around the balls for reassurance. "Peachy."

He runs his tongue over his lower lip. "Ladies first?"

I gulp in a breath. "How about together? You turn around and—"

"Sure." He spins on his heel, and I hear the loudest zipper opening in the history of sound.

Do cock rings require erections? If so, Dracula was clearly ready for action, because almost instantly, Vlad says, "I'm all set."

His phone lights up.

"No video." I pull out my own phone and launch the app.

He grunts his agreement and clicks something on his end.

Oh my. The balls begin vibrating inside me, and I nearly drop Precious.

Holy A-spot, this feels good.

Too good. Moaning in the same room with Vlad kind of good.

Must distract him.

Frantically, I activate the vibration on his toy.

Did the phone just shake in his hands?

The ball vibration increases.

I up his also.

He ups mine again.

Why didn't we sit? Or lie down?

My eyes begin to roll back, but I still manage to up his vibration one more notch.

When the orgasm smashes into me, I can't suppress a moan.

His back tenses.

My pelvic muscles spasm a few more times, then relax.

Oh, no. The Kegel balls slip out of me onto the living room floor and begin rolling.

Fuck. If he sees my slickness on those balls, I'll die.

"Close your eyes!" I shout. "And please don't ask why."

"Done." The word sounds like a grunt.

Good.

Without turning off his vibration, I stash Precious into my purse and sprint over to where the balls stopped—four feet in front of Vlad.

Giving him his privacy, I resist the strong urge to peek at Dracula as I bend to pick up the balls.

The darn things slip through my fingers and roll away.

Since it's hard to not look at his junk and chase them this way, I drop on all fours and chase after the toy like a predator hunting her prey.

Finally.

I grab the balls.

Nope.

They slip out of my grasp once more.

Did I have to lube them up so well?

Knees beginning to hurt, I crawl to where they stopped.

Yes! I snatch them and manage to keep a grip.

Then I see the legs in front of me.

I look up.

Yep.

I'm head to head with Dracula.

Chapter Twenty-Four

*W*ow.

I'm a tiny mouse in front of an anaconda.

This is how Mowgli must've felt when he first met Kaa.

Clutching onto my balls for dear life, I gulp down the gallon of saliva that my salivary glands suddenly spurt into my mouth.

Did I mention wow?

Dracula is beautiful in his engorged hugeness. Noticeably bigger than even Glurp, he might not fit in me, though it might be fun to try.

The ring squeezes and vibrates Dracula near the base, somehow accentuating the already-awesome sight.

Somewhere above me, Vlad grunts in pleasure.

Fuck. I forgot they're attached.

I start to back away—just as a white, creamy liquid shoots out of Dracula and lands on my cheek.

I blink in disbelief.

Did that just happen?

More gushes out.

I instinctively squeeze my eyes shut as the warm liquid lands on my forehead, the other cheek, nose, and chin.

A warm droplet lands on Pinky and two on the Brain.

Well, now I know what it's like for the porn stars in those bukkake videos. When Bob wanted to do this exact thing with me a while back, I refused, thinking it degrading. Now I'm not so sure. Maybe if—

"What are you doing there?" Vlad sounds like he's seen a ghost.

Crap. He must've finally opened his eyes.

Keeping my own blinkers shut lest my eyeballs get impregnated, I climb to my feet. My cheeks burn so hot I half expect the Dracula juices to sizzle, like egg whites on a skillet.

"Don't move." I hear him rush away.

Is he escaping? Taking a picture? Ordering takeout?

I hear him come back, and a strong hand cradles my head.

Well, that's nice.

"The water should be warm," he murmurs.

I dare not peek.

A paper towel touches my forehead.

Oh. He's cleaning me up. That's sweet, or as sweet as this can be, given the substance in question.

Speaking of the substance, is it too late for me to sneak a taste?

No. He'd see, and though most guys would find that hot, I'm not sure what the protocol is for when the guy in question is your boss squared.

"I'm sorry," he says when he's done with the area around my eyes. Despite his words, his voice is more than a little husky. "I'm not sure how this happened, but—"

"It wasn't your fault." I open my eyes and watch as he finishes wiping my cheeks and chin, then looks uncertainly at my cleavage.

"It's fine," I say, flushing impossibly hotter. "Go for it."

His pupils dilate as he dabs the few droplets from Pinky and the Brain.

I glance down.

He's zipped up Dracula, but there appears to be a new bulge there.

Useful, I guess, in case we decide to do more testing.

He balls up the dirty towel in his hand. "Just so you know, I'm clean. I got myself tested after the last relationship, and I haven't been with anyone since then, so—"

"I'm clean too," I blurt. "And on the pill."

His eyes gleam. "That's good to know, but the reason I told you about my medical history was so that you wouldn't worry about a herpes outbreak on your face. It wasn't quid pro quo."

Of course, that's what he meant. Stupid mouth. First it blurts TMI, now it wants to kiss him. Would he think it gross if I did kiss him? My mouth was spared the fountain of——

He dips his head and locks lips with me.

My heart goes supernova, and my knees threaten to buckle.

This is clearly a day of wows. His lips feel warm and soft and so good I nearly have another orgasm—and almost drop my balls. The room fades around me, and all my worries seem to evaporate. All my senses focus on the way his tongue gently strokes the inside of my mouth, the sweet, faintly minty warmth of his breath, the pounding of my pulse in my temples and——

He pulls away.

I'm breathing raggedly, and so is he.

"Why?" I ask breathlessly, staring up at him.

"We shouldn't." His voice is hoarse. "Still under the influence."

I draw back sharply. My arousal evaporates, replaced by an irrational surge of anger.

What the fuck is that supposed to mean? Is he saying he only kissed me because he had beer—or vodka—goggles on? Or does he think I can't make adult decisions with a mild buzz?

Before I can voice any of this, he has his phone out and is sending a text.

When the reply comes a millisecond later, he says, "Ivan will take you home. Come."

He herds me into the elevator, walks me down to the lobby, and holds open the limo door.

The ride home happens in a haze. A million questions loop through my mind, but two most of all: Why did he stop? And if a mere kiss was that amazing, how would it feel if we did more?

When I get home, I drop the balls into my sink and stare at myself in the mirror.

Ugh. My lopsided expression is a mix of curiosity, suspicion, and skepticism again. The glue on my left eyebrow wig must've given out at some point. At least I assume that's what happened. The thing is now missing, probably left in Vlad's towel.

No wonder he didn't want to do anything with me.

My first shower is scorching, the second one icy.

Jumping into my bed, I cover my head with a pillow and try to block out what happened.

Chapter Twenty-Five

*T*he first thing I do in the morning is check Precious for messages from Vlad.

Nope. Radio silence.

I check my work email next and find a message from Sandra, requesting yet another update. I ask her if she's okay doing it tomorrow. Until I hear from Vlad, I can't honestly tell her everything is on track.

There's also an email from Mike Ventura in my inbox—a.k.a. Butt-Head and maybe-Phantom:

Want to have that chat at 11:30 tomorrow?

As I think about it, Sandra replies that she's fine with my suggestion.

I set up a meeting with her for eleven and tell Mike I'm game for eleven-thirty. This way, I'll kill two birds/coworkers with one commute stone.

Precious dings with a text.

My heart leaps.

It's from Vlad.

Are you up yet?

Hand shaking, I reply with: *Yes. And no hangover. You?*

He calls me instead of replying via text.

"Hi," I say.

"Hi yourself."

I clear my throat. "Look, about yesterday—"

"Can we do the pig playdate today?" he asks at almost the same time. "Oracle looks lonely this morning."

I hesitate for only a second. "Of course. What time did—"

"We're on our way," he says. "Have you had breakfast?"

"Not yet."

"What would you like?"

Feeling a little surreal, I tell him I won't say no to some blueberry muffins.

"Have a snack for now," he says. "We'll be there soon."

"Sure," I say, but he's already hung up.

Crap.

I have to make myself presentable, pronto. At least my place is still clean from his last visit.

Attacking my makeup kit, I recall the eyebrow debacle from last night. Was it why he stopped kissing me or not? Either way, I use the temporary eyebrow tattoos as the second-best solution, then order another pair of eyebrow wigs for later, in case my own eyebrows don't make a reappearance soon enough.

Just as I'm wriggling into a clean pair of jeans, I get a call on Precious. I nearly trip as I dash to pick it up.

It could be Vlad.

Nope.

It's Ava. She demands an update, so I give it to her.

"Unbelievable," she says when I'm done. "How could two people give each other that many orgasms yet only get to first base?"

I roll my eyes. "Aren't sex toys third base? And aren't facials some kind of a base too?"

She chuckles. "All I'm saying is that you should've gone all the way."

I sigh. "I don't think he wanted me. He might find me repugnant."

Ava scoffs. "Repugnant? You? Are you—"

The doorbell rings.

"Got to go," I shout into the phone and hang up.

"Who is it?" I ask pointedly, approaching the door.

"Vlad," he says, a note of approval in his tone.

I open up.

Damn. Why do I always feel surprised by his looks?

Breathlessly, I take in his shaggy black locks—including the unruly one that makes my fingers itch to touch it—and the beautifully shaped lines of his lips. His eyes are the deepest shade of blue behind his horn-rimmed glasses, and he's wearing his Matrix-inspired getup. In one hand, he's holding Oracle in a carrier, and in the other, a brown bag.

I swallow my drool. "Please come in." I gesture toward my living room.

He takes his shoes off again, hangs up the trench coat by the door, and brings the carrier over to Monkey's house.

"Here." He hands me a muffin. "Mind if I put them into the play area?"

"Please." I attack the muffin with fervor.

Yum. He either stopped by the best bakery in NYC, or I'm very hungry.

As I eat, I watch Oracle and Monkey rub noses together.

"I brought them snacks too." Vlad takes out a green vegetable I've never seen before. "You mind?"

"Not at all. What is that?"

"Hop shoots." He bites a piece of his. "They're washed. You want to try?"

With a shrug, I taste the veg. It reminds me of kale, with a faintly nutty aftertaste. "This is good. Why have I never seen these in the supermarket? Or restaurants? Is it a special guinea pig crop?"

And if so, why did we just eat it?

He places a long shoot into the aquarium. "The process to harvest this stuff is elaborate, so they're a little pricey for most people."

Seeing the shoot, Oracle grabs it and starts nibbling.

Monkey tastes it from the other side, and must

love it because she begins pulling on the green stem pretty vigorously.

Almost violently.

In return, Oracle pulls on her end.

Monkey keeps pulling on hers.

It becomes a hilarious tug of war—at least hilarious for me.

Vlad actually frowns. "I forgot how much Oracle likes those things. I might've inadvertently created friction."

He's right.

After they rip the plant in half and finish eating it, Oracle begins to chase Monkey around—with squealing throughout.

When she finally corners Monkey, she mounts her and begins to hump.

Huh, okay. When Vlad mentioned friction a second ago, I didn't think it would be of the sexual kind. But why humping? They're both female, so wouldn't it make more sense if one went down on the other, or—and I'm not sure if their bodies are built for it—they could try something like scissoring.

"You said Oracle was a she," I say, suppressing a laugh as the humping intensifies. "Doesn't this require boy parts?"

"It's about dominance." He tosses two pieces of the veg in two different corners of the aquarium.

As if to confirm his words, Monkey sprints out from under Oracle, makes a loop, and begins trying to make her friend her bitch.

"Guinea pigs must be sexist," I say, grinning. "Why is the one who gets humped the less dominant one? And shouldn't that only apply in the bedroom anyway, not to who gets more snacks?"

He returns my grin. "And yet, how funny would it be if people tried this in boardrooms?"

We watch as the two guinea pigs eventually tire of trying to hump each other and just eat a hop shoot each.

"I think it's a truce," Vlad says. "Neither is trying to steal from the other."

"Where can I get that hop shoots stuff?" I ask. "Monkey clearly loves it."

"My dad has a hookup." Vlad drops more of the veg in front of the two piggies. "But as I said, it's a little pricey."

I eye the nondescript vegetable. "How much can it be?"

"With Dad's discount, four hundred per pound," he says with a straight face.

A *little* pricey?

I gape at the guinea pigs, then at him. "Seriously?"

He nods.

"And will they lay a golden egg now?"

He chuckles. "Not likely."

I shake my head. "That's like feeding a cat caviar."

A grin flashes across his face. "My mom did that with her cat, and only stopped because it apparently made the kitty litter too smelly."

Holy cow. "I must not be a good pet owner," I say. "I wouldn't dream of getting Monkey a vegetable that costs more than a pair of shoes."

He hands me another hop shoot. "Would you get it for yourself?"

I taste it again. "Nope. Not unless I was sick, and this was the only cure. Actually, in that case, I'd get it for Monkey too. As medicine."

"Well, don't worry." He dumps the remainder of the snack into the aquarium. "I'll bring more to all the play dates, so Monkey will continue to enjoy this."

Aww. He wants the girls to have more play dates. And, as a side effect, he's willing to spend more time with me.

This might be a great time to bring up yesterday.

"Listen," I say, proud that I'm actually going for it. "There's something I wanted to ask."

He gives me his full attention.

I blush.

The words don't come out.

I guess this is mission abort. I'm clearly chickening out.

"What is it?" he asks, now looking a little concerned.

"The testing," I blurt in desperation. "Since you're here, and we're now okay doing it face to face, I was wondering if you wanted to be productive."

Eck. I almost said "reproductive" there at the end.

He looks thoughtful.

Crapo. If he thinks I'm repulsive, he'll come up with an excuse not to do it.

"Of course," he says. "Let's."

I guess that's good, but this doesn't definitively prove anything. He might be just doing this for his sis.

A way to tell might be to watch him closely during the testing, see if he enjoys watching me.

My blush deepens. "Do you want to do it now?"

He glances at the guinea pigs. They're back to being best buds and are enthusiastically grooming each other. "Sure."

I run to my bedroom and come back with the genitalia-decorated suitcase. Opening it wide on the floor by the couch, I contemplate my choices.

His expression is guarded as he examines the suitcase with me.

Beginning to lose my nerve, I point at a large wand-type vibrator. "How about that one?" As I speak, my heart rate skyrockets, and I have to remind myself that I've just chosen the least naughty toy of the bunch. They sell these things at Target under the guise of "massager."

Hell, my mom got me one like this once. She called it the Vibronator.

"Sounds good." His gaze lifts from the suitcase to my face. "Should I be looking away, like yesterday?"

It would be hard to tempt him if he turns, but I don't have the balls to undress either, so I say, "How about I use it over my jeans? It should be powerful enough to work that way."

Looking unsure, he gets the device out.

Is he wondering if he should be the one to hold the thing in place for me? Do I want him to?

"Here." He hands it to me, much to my disappointment. "I'll get the app ready."

As he plays with his phone, I lie back on the couch and spread my legs a little—just enough to be seductive yet still believable as the position necessary to get the vibration job done.

When he looks back at me, his breath seems to hitch.

Score.

I feel a sudden boost of courage.

"Here." I pat the couch next to me. "Things didn't go well the last time we did this standing."

He sits down next to me, the sensual notes of his cologne teasing my nostrils as he murmurs, "Let me know when Mina is ready."

"Mina?" Has he forgotten that I'm Fanny? And why am I in third person all of a sudden?

His sexy lips quirk. "Mina was Dracula's romantic interest. I figured since you named mine, I'd help you name yours."

Holy vampirism. He's beyond perfect. None of my exes ever played along, finding my penchant for nicknames silly.

Doing my best to hide my glee, I lift one of my temporary eyebrow tattoos. "You should leave all the nicknaming to me. Mina is a terrible one."

He lifts an eyebrow. "Go ahead then, rename it."

Hmm, a challenge.

I hope I can rise to it. Between having never named that part of myself and all the adrenaline, I'm drawing a blank. Then it comes to me. "How about Gizmo?"

He shoots a glance at my crotch. "Like an electronic device one wants to play with?"

I grin. "No. Like the cute creature from the Gremlins. You know… dangerous if wet."

He groans, and we both burst out laughing.

When we stop, he shows me his ready-to-go screen. "Shall I?"

Still high from all the laughter, I feel extra bold. "I was wondering if you could hold the wand for me."

His smile disappears. "You sure?"

My face is on fire, but I nod. "Please." I hand the wand to him.

He activates it through the app, and it roars like a chainsaw in my palm before he snatches it away.

I gulp in a deep breath.

It's happening.

Holy wandness, it's happening.

He puts down his phone, then leans in and slowly presses the loudly vibrating toy against my jeans.

The air whooshes out of my lungs. Even through the layers, the vibration is insane—and brings me to an orgasm almost instantly, dragging a loud moan out of me.

His pupils dilate, and I see he's about to pull the wand away, so I clasp his wrist to keep it there. I'm greedy for another orgasm, which I can already feel building. The tension is coiling low in my core, my skin tingling as my nipples harden in the confines of my bra.

His face is a mask of purely male satisfaction, even as his eyes are heavy-lidded with arousal.

The orgasm crashes over me, making me cry out. It's shameless, bold, but I don't care. I like how this is affecting him. There's a huge bulge in his pants, mere inches away from me.

Should I unzip him and unleash Dracula?

Not yet.

For now, I grab his other hand and place it over Pinky, bucking my hips against the wand to intensify the sensations that are mercilessly building again.

His eyes darken, and he squeezes my flesh appreciatively, just as another orgasm rocks me, making me scrunch my eyes shut and moan yet again.

As the aftershocks fade, I open my eyes—and stare right into my parents' faces.

Chapter Twenty-Six

*D*o orgasms make you hallucinate?

Wait, no, they appear to be real.

Holy fuck.

Mom and Dad have barged into my apartment yet again.

Stiffening, Vlad yanks the vibrator away from my crotch area as I gape at my grinning parental units, painfully aware of the open suitcase of toys at my feet and the orgasm they must've just witnessed.

"That is simply fabulous, my dear!" Mom sounds positively giddy. "I knew the Vibronator would come in handy."

I leap to my feet, and so does Vlad. Swiftly deactivating the wand, he tosses it into the suitcase and closes the thing shut.

I debate whether to die on the spot or not. Pretty sure people have fallen on a sword for much less dishonor.

At least my orgasm-flushed face can't get any redder.

Somehow, I recover my tongue. "Mom, Dad, this is Vlad." I'm proud of the steadiness of my voice. "Vlad, these are my parents. They've clearly never learned about boundaries."

Coolly composed now, Vlad extends a hand to Mom. "Nice to meet you, Mrs. Pack."

Mom looks on the verge of drooling. "Please call me Venus."

"Of course, Venus," Vlad says and extends a hand in greeting to my dad. "Mr. Pack, it's great to meet you as well."

"Call me Wolf," Dad says, and it's clear he's also impressed by Vlad, though unlike Mom, he doesn't look like he's about to jump him, cougar style.

My embarrassment eases slightly.

Time for payback.

"You heard that right," I tell Vlad. "He's a one-man Wolf Pack, like that guy in *The Hangover*. Grand-parents named him that as a prank, and these two played an even worse prank on me."

"Great to meet you, Wolf," Vlad says, showing no sign that he heard what I said.

In general, he's handling this much, much better than I would've if his parents had barged in on us.

Mom beams at Vlad. "We came to drag Fanny to lunch. Would you like to join us?"

"I'd love to," Vlad says without hesitation.

Wait, what is this now? Lunch with my parents *and* Vlad? We're not at the "meeting the parents" stage.

We're still in the limbo stage.

Then again, I kind of met his too.

Could we do this any more backward?

"What kind of food do you like?" Dad asks Vlad.

"I'm not picky," he replies.

Dad proposes a laundry list of cuisines, and he and Mom debate where they want to go as though Vlad and I are not even in the room. As they go on, I sneak a glance at Vlad's poker face.

I have no idea what he's thinking about the two intruders.

Mom and Dad were the first people I tested my app on. My code determined that Mom looks like Princess Fiona from Shrek, but, spoiler alert, after she turns permanently into an ogre. Dad matched with Garfield—and that might be why Monkey is absolutely terrified of him.

"What do you think of sushi?" Mom asks Vlad.

He places a hand on my shoulder. "I go where Fanny goes."

Spying the hand, Mom exchanges a knowing glance with Dad. "The food Fanny likes is too plain."

"Hey, I eat sushi," I say, trying and failing not to sound indignant.

Mom chuckles. "In Japan, they serve California rolls in the American food restaurants, along with burgers."

I narrow my eyes. "I get other stuff too. How about we go, and I'll let you order for me?"

Mom claps her hands in excitement, and I herd everyone out of the apartment.

My phone pings.

I sneak a peek at it.

It's a text from Vlad:

Want to take the limo, or walk to a great little place nearby?

Did he type that in his pocket?

"Mom, Dad, Vlad knows a great little sushi place nearby," I say. "What do you think?"

They gladly agree to a walk, and we set out on our journey, with Mom and Dad quizzing us about how we met and how long we've been dating.

"We work together," Vlad replies, unflappable as always. "How about the two of you? How long have you been married?"

The diversion works. Mom launches into the story I wish I'd never heard, and especially not the dozens of times she's told it in my presence. Apparently, she replied to an ad in the newspaper and posed nude for Dad's painting, he found her irresistible, and one thing led to another, by which I mean that they covered each other in paint and had wild sex on a giant canvas. The resulting work of art actually hangs in their living room to this day.

If I ever get therapy, I'm sure I'll bring it up. A lot.

Vlad listens to this inappropriate story as calmly as if she'd told him they'd met on eHarmony.

Then another text from him arrives:

Do you want me to have Ivan buy you a keychain lock for the door?

Is he afraid the next time they'll barge in, they'll start making art at my place?

Grinning, I reply in the affirmative.

How about one of those smart video doorbells? I know a brand that's extra safe, privacy-wise.

As I agree to this too, we reach the restaurant and walk in.

"Konnichiwa," the restaurant staff yells at us in unison.

Vlad replies in kind, his pronunciation sounding flawless to me.

I catch Mom and Dad exchanging an approving glance.

We get seated, and Mom orders me a sushi deluxe, then gets the same for herself and Dad. Vlad orders his sushi à la carte, naming the pieces by their Japanese names like a pro.

"So, Venus, I heard you sing opera," Vlad says when the waitress leaves. He pulls out his phone. "Would I be able to find a performance by you online?"

She bobs her head enthusiastically. "Search my name, but ignore all the packs of razors and razor blades that pop up early on in the search."

Two seconds later, Mom's mezzo-soprano emanates from Vlad's phone's speakers.

"Ah," Vlad says after barely two beats of music. "*The Habanera* from *Carmen*."

"Marry him," Mom says in a very loud whisper.

My face matches the red top of the full-sodium soy sauce.

Facing Vlad, Mom asks, "What is that wonderful accent I detect in your speech?"

"Russian," Vlad says. "Speaking of, have you been in anything by Tchaikovsky? *The Queen of Spades* is my favorite of his."

The food comes as they launch into an animated discussion of Russian opera, and one thing becomes clear to me: no matter what happens between us, Mom will never, ever, stop talking about Vlad.

"Wolf, you're a painter, right?" Vlad asks when Mom's mouth becomes busy with a piece of fatty tuna.

And just like that, Dad and Vlad are soon dropping names like *Repin* and *Malevich* as they talk Russian art.

I eat my sushi and enjoy most of it. However, there are two pieces of something brown I've never had before, and they look particularly unappetizing.

"That's *uni*," Vlad says, noticing where my chopsticks are hovering. "It's sea urchin gonads."

Of course it is. Still, that's a better name than what I had in my head: poopy sushi.

I'm determined to be adventurous, though.

I eat a piece of pickled ginger to cleanse my palate, then dip the tip of my chopstick into the brown substance and lick it gingerly.

It's creamy in a gross way and much too briny for my taste.

There's no way I'm eating it.

Grr. Now Mom will get to say, "I told you so." Which is unfair, because I ate all the other stuff, raw fish included.

"You know, that's my favorite," Vlad says, noticing my grimace. "Can we please trade?"

I squeeze his knee gratefully and put the uni on his plate, grabbing a piece of his salmon and yellow fish in exchange.

"Uni is considered an aphrodisiac in Japan," Mom whispers to Vlad conspiratorially.

If that's true, given the way she flirts with Vlad, she must've eaten a whole ocean of urchin gonads for breakfast.

"Have you been to Japan?" she asks Vlad.

Here we go. When I was in college, my parents started to travel, and now they never shut up about it— and about the fact that other than my one and only trip to Prague, I haven't been anywhere outside the US.

It's another dig at my unadventurousness. Which is unfair. I simply haven't had the time or the funds to travel at this stage of my career.

I would totally go lots of places if I could.

Probably.

I hope.

Vlad nods. "Kyoto was my favorite city, but I've been all over the country."

Mom grins. "Us too. Everything was matcha-flavored in Kyoto. Did you go to the Monkey Park?"

They bond over Japan for a while before switching focus to Russia, which they quiz Vlad about. It's a destination they haven't crossed off their bucket list. I listen as he gladly answers their questions, telling them all about his hometown of Murmansk and how one can see the Northern Lights there in the winter.

I have to admit, I would kill to see those.

The aurora borealis phenomenon is definitely on *my* bucket list.

We finish off the meal with fried green tea ice cream that, according to Mom, "isn't as good as the ones you can get in Kyoto."

When the check comes, Vlad grabs it and hands his card to the waiter before my dad can so much as open his mouth about splitting the bill.

"Thank you," Mom tells him as we walk out of the restaurant and head back to my place.

The Russian quiz continues during our walk home. As we reach my building, Vlad stops and smiles warmly at my parents.

"It was very nice to meet you both," he says. "Would you like a ride home?"

They look confused until he gestures at the limo.

Mom gives him her cougariest onceover of the day. "Yes, please. Thank you."

We walk over to the limo, where Vlad takes a large backpack from Ivan and says something in Russian, nodding at my folks.

Ivan dips his head in agreement and holds the door for Mom and Dad as they scooch in.

"Bye," I say with a wave. "Call before you come over next time."

The limo pulls away, and I let out a sigh. "They won't call."

Vlad unzips the backpack. "This should help."

Inside the bag is a drill, a keychain, and a box with, presumably, the video doorbell.

When we get to my door, I watch Vlad install it all in a matter of minutes—an unexpected display of handyman abilities that's a stronger aphrodisiac than urchin gonads.

Once the doorbell is set up and I have the prerequisite app running on Precious, Vlad says, "Let's test it."

I go inside and flip on the new keychain, leaving him on the doorstep.

He rings the doorbell.

Precious shows me his gorgeous face.

"Yep. It works." I open the lock but not the keychain.

He tries to open the door, but the keychain thwarts him.

"Great." I let him in for real, my heartbeat speeding up as I prepare to be bold once again. Looking him in the eyes, I say as steadily as I can manage, "Now we should probably resume the *other* kind of testing."

His face goes taut. "You sure?"

Instead of an answer, I lead him into the living room and open the suitcase again.

Like one of Pavlov's dogs, I'm already salivating at the promise of more orgasms.

"I almost forgot." Vlad takes out a small bundle of lacy cloth from his pocket. "You left this in my bathroom."

Holy crap. I forgot my underwear at his house and didn't even realize it.

Cheeks going nuclear, I snatch the panties out of his hand. "Sorry about that. Had to leave in a rush and all."

"About that." He steps closer, his eyes impossibly blue behind the lenses of his glasses. "I hope you're okay."

Okay? What is he—oh. All the warm fuzzies leave me as I recall last night and the way he so abruptly pulled away.

"Was it because I looked like a freak?" I blurt.

His brow furrows. "What are you talking about?"

"We kissed. You pulled away. You thought I looked like a freak, right?" I gesture at my fake eyebrows.

His expression shifts from confusion to unmistakable desire, his lids lowering as his eyes sweep hungrily over my body. Stepping up to me, he cradles my face in his broad palms. "Fannychka…" His voice is rough velvet. "You'd be beautiful without a single hair on your head."

Oh. My. God. If I were a computer, system error

messages would be blaring through my speakers. As is, my heart hammers, and every hair on my body stands on end, as if an electric current is running under my skin.

I. Am. So. Turned. On.

"You had vodka in your system," he continues without letting me go. "And I—" He takes a deep breath. "I want your mind clear when you beg me to fuck you."

Wow. Now the computer would explode.

I was not expecting to hear those words come out of his mouth—and now that they have, the images dancing in my mind are beyond X-rated.

And hot.

So scorching hot that I seem to have lost my tongue.

"Beg?" I finally manage to squeeze out.

A cocky grin tugs at his sensual lips. "I guess you can also just ask. Nicely."

"Nicely?"

"Good enough," he murmurs and dips his head, slanting his lips across mine.

Holy overactive ovaries. Now I feel like someone has taken the little bits of the exploded computer and began putting the pieces back together, paying special attention to the erogenous zones.

The kiss is hungrier than the one last night.

More primal.

My knees start to feel weak.

He must notice. Still kissing me, he backs me

toward the couch, and as I plop backward onto it, he leans over me, lips brushing my ear as he murmurs roughly, "I wanted to bend you over the table at Starbucks when I first saw you."

Error. Error. Hormone overload. Speaking functions compromised. Reboot required.

Losing my head completely, I ball his shirt in my fist and drag him on top of me.

The coiled muscles press firmly against my body.

We resume kissing.

My hand slides through his thick, silky hair.

He nibbles on my lip.

I suck on his tongue.

Steam collects between my skin and clothes. I want them off, so I begin to unbutton my shirt.

He leans slightly back, pupils dilating impossibly wide.

I slip out of my top.

He rips his shirt clean off, sending buttons flying like bullets across the room. Left in a white t-shirt, he strips that off too.

Video buffer overrun. Graphics card overclocked.

Vlad must spend serious time at the gym. That or his body was sculpted in ancient Greece. The hardquilted muscles gleam with beads of sweat, and I want to lick them all off.

He unbuttons my bra, releasing Pinky and the Brain from their prison.

"Beautiful." He cups Pinky, and my nipple practically stabs his palm.

Can you go crazy from lust? I need him inside me so much I think I might scream.

Kissing his neck, I slide my tongue over his pecs, down the washboard abs and lower, toward the landing strip of hair below his navel. At the same time, I unzip his pants.

Holy hell.

Dracula is almost bursting out of his underwear.

Vlad kicks off his pants, then peels my jeans off.

"You okay?" he asks, eyes hooded.

I pull down my panties in my reply.

After this, I dare anyone to call me unadventurous.

"Beautiful." His voice comes out guttural, cave-man-like.

He straddles me, his naked skin rubbing over mine.

I can't believe this is happening.

He kisses my neck, then sucks on my nipple before languidly dragging his tongue over my belly and lower. And lower still, with mind-numbing, teasing slowness.

After what feels like forever, I feel his warm breath on my sex.

Division by zero. File not found.

He gives it a probing lick.

I cry out.

Belka's squishy Space Age material has nothing on his swirling, clever tongue. So clever, it should get an honorary PhD from Harvard.

The pressure builds.

I knead my hands in his hair, arching up as the pressure grows unbearable, intensifying with each passing second.

With a loud moan, I blast apart.

He looks up, primal male satisfaction written all over his beautiful face. "More?"

"Lie down." My words come out boldly, almost like a command. There's no room for shyness in the desire gripping me.

He gladly obeys.

I pull down his underwear, unleashing Dracula.

Input device driver error. Allocate more space.

Cautiously, I give his shaft an ice cream lick.

He twitches in response, urging me on.

I slide all of him into my mouth, jaws stretching to the limit.

"Fuck," Vlad grunts above me.

Taking that as encouragement, I make a circle with my tongue.

And another.

After a third, he pulls away. "I don't want to finish like that." His voice is hoarse, his breathing uneven. "I want to be inside you. Assuming you're ready for that."

Ready?

If I don't get him in me, I might die.

There's just one problem.

"I don't have a condom." I glance around the living room as though looking for the latex fairy.

His eyes roam ravenously over my body. "Me neither. This whole development is a little unexpected."

I dart a glance at his erection. "You said you're clean."

His breath hitches, voice roughening further. "You did too. And you're on the pill."

"So are you. I mean, I *am* on the pill. The only one on the pill."

Ugh, why am I babbling? And flushing again?

Instead of responding, he lifts me up and manhandles me until we switch places, with me sprawled on the couch and him on top, Dracula against my belly.

His lips slant over mine once more, and as I return the kiss, I feel his wicked fingers enter me.

Whoa.

I gasp into his mouth as he locates my G-spot with a precision Glurp would be jealous of, then gives it a light rub.

I come undone with a scream.

Eyes heavy-lidded, he brings his fingers to his mouth and licks them clean. "Delicious."

His fingers leave a gnawing emptiness that needs to be filled.

Time to take my daring to the ultimate level.

I wrap my hand around Dracula and slowly guide him into me.

Input device connected. Error. Reboot imminent.

Vlad's face looks strained as I take him in by small increments, letting my muscles adjust.

Okay. I *can* take him. I was worried for a second.

"You okay?" he grunts when Dracula is rooted as deeply as he can go.

I manage a small nod.

He begins to thrust, lightly at first.

I moan.

He speeds up.

My nails dig into his back.

The thrusts intensify, yet it's not enough.

I crave more.

Harder.

Deeper.

Sliding my hands to his glutes, I arch up, impaling myself as I tip over the edge.

My toes curl as I scream his name.

As my pelvic muscles tremble around Dracula, Vlad grunts in pleasure. I feel him harden, and then there's the warm sensation of his release—which brings me to yet another climax.

"Fuck." He hugs me tight, his chest heaving against mine. "That was remarkable." Realizing he might smother me, he pushes up on one elbow.

Smiling into his face, I rub my nose against his, channeling my inner guinea pig. "Merely remarkable?"

"Amazing. Mind-blowing." He grins. "Better?"

"A good start." I wriggle out from under him and

jump to my feet. "Keep talking as you join me in the shower."

Giggling, I run into the bathroom, and as he chases me, he peppers me with enough positive adjectives to fill a thesaurus.

Once inside, I set the shower water to a comfy temperature and get under the stream.

He looks me over hungrily, then steps in, taking up all the freaking space.

Before I can object, he begins to lather me sensuously.

Okay, I guess all is forgiven.

Once I'm squeaky clean, I return the favor, covering every one of his copious muscles with soap.

"You know," I say as I lather his washboard abs. "If I wanted to be mean to *my* kid, I'd call her or him Six."

He grins. "Six Pack. That *is* pretty wicked."

When the shower is done, we wrap ourselves in towels and return to the living room.

"Your shirt is toast." I kick the buttonless mess with a bare foot.

He shrugs. "I can wear the t-shirt."

He'll actually look casual for a change? The universe just might implode.

Seeing him with that towel turns me on again, and my newfound boldness shows no signs of abating.

"What should we do now?" I ask, glancing at the suitcase.

Did Dracula just stir under that towel?

Vlad smirks. "What did you have in mind?"

"There are toys we haven't tested yet." I fake innocence by batting my eyelashes at him. "I, for one, think that's an oversight that needs fixing."

He unwraps his towel to reveal Dracula ready for action.

Insatiable much?

I love it.

Giddily, I choose a toy to use on him—and bring him to another climax. Then he returns the favor many times over since there are more female-oriented toys.

Countless orgasms later, we run out of toys, and my stomach growls.

"How unladylike." I spank my belly before wriggling into my underwear and jeans.

"We better feed the beast." He takes out his phone. "What are you in the mood for?"

"Pizza?"

He nods approvingly. "One of the best places in the country is just a few blocks away."

———

The thin crust pizza is out of this world, and we devour it over beers and a good conversation. Among other things, we learn each other's ages—he's thirty-two to my twenty-four—and when each other's birthday is, a topic that leads into a discussion about our mutual skepticism regarding Zodiac signs.

When our dinner is done, we feed the other beasts —Oracle and Monkey.

Once our pets are happy pigs, Vlad and I cuddle on the couch and watch *The Matrix*. As the movie plays, I try not to think about the implications of what's just happened and just enjoy the moment. Because if I do think about it, I will freak out.

Because I just slept with Vlad.

With my boss's boss.

The computer will definitely crash if I go there.

Instead, I focus on the movie. We say our favorite lines together with the characters and, in some rare cases, complain about something we think could've been done better.

For example, why did the machines use humans as batteries when guinea pigs would've required a much simpler virtual reality prison to keep them content?

"I think the original reason the machines needed humans was as a computational substrate," Vlad says. "That seemed too complex of an idea for the general public, so it was dumbed down to batteries. Or maybe it was just product placement."

I grin at him. "I bet you're right."

"This always bugged me," he says when Trinity quips the classic "Dodge this" line and shoots the agent in the head. "Given how fast the agents can move, she wouldn't have had the time to finish the words before he'd have thwarted her."

I vehemently shake my head. "When a line is that cool, you need to just relax and not overthink it."

He laughs and we finish the rest of the movie without comments. Then we stream the sequels, complaining more often as we do.

"I should head out," he says when the credits on the last of the trilogy roll on the screen.

Still on my bravery high, I say, "If you want, you can stay here."

Turns out, he very much likes the idea of staying, so we make our way to the bedroom, where I promptly end up on all fours.

"That was even better than before," he murmurs huskily when we're both just limp noodles on my bed.

My oversexed grin is goofy. "You know, if we were guinea pigs, you'd officially be the dominant one after that."

His chuckle morphs into a yawn.

"Spoon me." It comes out bossier than I planned, but he grins and does it.

Before I know it, I fall asleep like that.

Cuddled securely in his arms.

Chapter Twenty-Seven

I feel warm and cozy and only partially awake.

Sometimes sleep is like a computer reboot for my brain, and this morning, this is truer than ever—I'm certainly having thoughts that have hidden in my subconscious until now.

It's insane how close I feel to Vlad.

Also—and maybe this is me being delusional—I feel like I know him. Know the real him, not the Impaler mask everyone at the office fears.

In fact, in barely no time at all, I've begun to feel that the two of us fit together like a set of nesting matryoshka dolls.

I grin as I think back on us cuddling on my couch. It was the best evening I can recall having. And the sex was the most mind-blowing of my life.

In fact, I might've had more orgasms yesterday than the entire year prior.

Most importantly, I've never felt this kind of connection with a guy. My longest relationship was Bob, and in the year we dated, I don't think I knew him this well, or felt like we fit this well, or enjoyed the intimacy, or—

Shit.

Could I be falling for Vlad?

A jolt of adrenaline banishes the remnants of drowsiness.

Falling for him could be a disaster. He might not feel the same—and he's my boss squared.

Crap.

I actually slept with the head of the company.

If anyone found out, they'd accuse me of sleeping my way to the top—or into the development department. And what if I do get moved or promoted for a reason other than merit?

Ugh. These would've been good things to consider before taking off my panties. In my defense, he had his shirt off by that point, and I'm only flesh and blood.

I open my eyes.

Vlad isn't in bed with me.

Forget the boss angle. My fear now is that last night meant nothing to him.

The scent of something fried and delicious reaches my nostrils.

I jackknife to my feet.

Maybe Vlad isn't gone after all?

I sprint to the bathroom to make myself presentable.

Interesting. I have a five-o-clock shadow. In the eyebrow area—not my cheeks. The temporary tattoos are holding on too, but given this growth spurt, I won't need them in a few days.

Teeth brushed and makeup applied, I put on some clothes and rush into the kitchen.

It *is* Vlad.

His back is to me, and he's only wearing pants.

Those back muscles make him look like a rower or a swimmer.

Drool forms in my mouth, only in part due to the smells of the fried goodness he's working on.

He should cook completely naked next time.

Wait, no. That could expose Dracula to hot oil burns.

I loudly clear my throat.

He turns around. "Ah. The sleepy kitten has risen. When I got up, I accidentally made a lot of noise, yet you didn't even twitch."

I grin. "I'm not a light sleeper."

He nods at the pan. "I hope you like your eggs over easy."

Over easy?

Is that subliminal messaging? Is he saying we're over or I'm easy?

He quirks an eyebrow. "A frown at my egg choice? How about I take this batch, and you tell me how you want yours done?"

Did I frown? Crapo. "Scrambled, please."

"Very American. Sit." He gestures at the table.

I obediently plop down next to a chair that has a man's shirt draped over it—a shirt with buttons that are attached, meaning it's not the one from yesterday.

"Where did you get a change of clothes?" I ask.

"Ivan brought it, along with the groceries." He turns back to the stove. "There were cobwebs in your fridge."

Great, Ivan knows Vlad stayed here.

Actually, Ivan, being his driver, would know either way.

Still, my cheeks warm. Though I've never done the walk of shame, I bet it feels a little like this.

He makes small talk as I drum my fingers on the table, debating if I should just flat-out ask him what he thinks is going on between us.

I should.

And will.

Any moment now.

His back is turned. That makes it easier, doesn't it?

Nope.

Not happening.

I must've used up all my boldness and bravery yesterday.

Mouth watering beyond reason, I watch as Vlad slaps the contents of the skillet on a plate, then cracks another egg, puts a little bit of milk in, and stirs.

Damn. Who would've thought such domestic

minutiae could be this hot? I feel my brain scrambling along with that egg.

How weird would it be if I played with myself here at the breakfast table?

Or if I got a toy?

"Here." He scrapes the skillet onto another plate and brings the yumminess to the table, along with a bottle of ketchup.

I attack my food. After the exertions of last night, my appetite is through the roof.

"It's eight forty-five," I say when the worst of my hunger is satiated. "You're legendary for being in your office at the crack of dawn. What gives?"

He shrugs. "The beauty of not having a boss is that I get up when I want."

"I bet that's nice." I shovel more egg into my mouth. "How did you end up owning your own company in the first place?"

He smiles. "After college, I worked for Bloomberg for a bit. Since I lived with parents, I was able to save a little money. When I realized that I needed to run things myself if I didn't want to go mad, I asked my parents for a loan to help me start Binary Birch. The rest is history."

"Impressive," I say, attacking the rest of my eggs. And I mean it, too. To own a successful software company at thirty-two years of age is no small feat.

"What are your plans for the day?" he asks.

I swallow the eggs in my mouth. "Write up Belka testing results. Meet with Sandra to give her the good news—and hopefully get new work. After that, I have a meeting with Mike Ventura."

He frowns. "Ventura? Why?"

Is that jealousy I hear in his voice?

"Code chat," I say.

"I see," he says, the frown going away. "You know, if you have any programming questions, you can talk to me. I might know a thing or two Ventura doesn't."

"I'll take you up on that now that I know." I grin impishly at him. "Would you like me to cancel the meeting with Mike?"

He spears the last of his food. "It's fine. Ventura is a decent coder. I doubt his advice can do much harm."

I take our empty plates and carry them to the sink. "What about you? Big plans for the day?"

To my deep disappointment, he begins putting on his shirt. "Meetings. Krav Maga training. Lunch with you, assuming you're willing."

Huh. Is Krav Maga how he got so in shape?

"I think I *might* be available for lunch." My eager grin makes it difficult to play coy.

"Good. Mind if I leave Oracle here?" He gestures at the aquarium. "After I fed them, she and Monkey had a blast playing."

"Of course she can stay."

Especially since that guarantees you have to come get her.

And maybe stay over again.

And—

"Come lock the door behind me," he says.

I follow him there.

He puts on his shoes.

I suddenly feel shy. "Bye?"

"No." He leans down and gives me the hottest goodbye kiss of my life. When he straightens, there's a purely male smirk on his lips. "Now it's a bye."

Closing the door, I fan myself.

That man will turn me into a sex addict.

My steps are light as I prance back to the living room. Opening my laptop, I finalize the testing documentation—reddening at my recollection as I type.

When I'm done, I check on the pigs. They're grooming each other, happy as clams at a vegan restaurant.

Since my meeting with Sandra is getting closer, I set out on my commute to the office.

Chapter Twenty-Eight

*A*s we settle in the meeting room, Sandra doesn't meet my gaze.

Weird.

Does she think I'm about to disappoint her?

"I have good news," I say, and tell her the testing is completed.

"That's great," she says, still not meeting my eyes. "I'm sure Mr. Chortsky will be pleased."

Did she wince at the last bit?

What the hell is this about?

"I'm ready for other projects now," I say. "Do you have anything interesting for me to test?"

She finally looks at me. "This is a little sudden. Let me have a think, and I'll get back to you."

Okay. I guess I did ambush her with being done with this project so quickly. Still, I can't help but feel she's behaving oddly.

"How are things with you in general?" I ask.

Maybe something is up with her health?

She stands up. "Everything's great. I have another meeting, though, so I better run."

Okay, whatever.

I wait for her to leave and check the time.

Still a few minutes before my meeting with Mike.

Going to the pantry, I make tea, wondering the entire time if Vlad is going to catch me here again.

Or rather, hoping he does.

Nope. Tea finished, with no Vlad in sight.

I get to the meeting room early and sip another cup of tea as I check for new messages from Phantom. If Mike turns out to be my mystery mentor, it would be polite to be up to speed on his wisdom.

Turns out Phantom was too busy to write.

Oh, well. Maybe like me, he had a busy Monday.

I pull out the work phone to check my email, but before I do, the meeting room door opens, and Butt-Head—I mean, Mike—waltzes in.

With a wide grin, he passes by a dozen chairs before plopping into the one right next to me.

Is everyone acting weird today, or is something up with me?

"Where's your laptop?" I put my phone down on the table. "I didn't bring mine."

"Laptop?" He gapes at me like I've sprouted a pink mohawk.

I eye him in confusion. "Don't we need a screen to look at code?"

He slides the chair closer to me. "Actually, I have a

confession to make. It wasn't code I wanted to talk to you about."

Why do I have a bad feeling about this?

I shift my chair away. "What then?"

He leans in, and I can smell stale coffee and even staler garlic on his breath. "Rumor has it, you're using the guys around the office to test sex toys—and I want to throw my name in the hat."

Chapter Twenty-Nine

*M*y eyes all but pop out of their sockets. "What?"

He frowns. "I thought we had a moment there, in the elevator. Or do you only invite people who can help your career?"

I jackknife to my feet, my face burning as if from a slap. "This conversation is over."

He jumps up and grabs my elbow. "Hey. I'm in dev. You want to move over there. I'm sure I could help."

I give him a scathing glare. "Let me go."

"Come on. Don't be like that." His grip tightens. "I just—"

"Let. Go. Of. Her."

The voice is pure Impaler.

Mike loosens his grip instantly.

Vlad is in the doorway, his gaze trained on my assailant.

If looks could kill, Mike's body would be a blood-less husk.

Paling, Mike looks from me to Vlad. "I was just—"

Before I can even blink, Vlad is between me and Mike. "Get out."

Mike takes a shuffling step back. "I just wanted to be a tester, like you."

Vlad takes a menacing step toward his employee. "You're fired. Effective immediately."

For a second, Mike looks shell-shocked—as though the concept of getting fired for harassing a female coworker is rocket science to him. In the next moment, anger replaces the shock on his face. "How convenient. A spot opens on the dev team just as your mistress wants it."

"You're trespassing." Vlad's voice is guttural and frightening. "One more word, and you will be force-fully removed from the premises." His powerful fists clench and unclench at his sides.

Mike pales further, his bravado deflating. Turning on his heel, he scurries out of the room.

Vlad strides over to the phone in the middle of the table and orders security to make sure he leaves the building and never comes back.

As he does that, I finally recover from shock enough to start putting the pieces together.

A rumor. About my testing.

Was that why Sandra had acted so weird? Had she also heard about said rumor?

And what a strange one it is. Me testing with a bunch of men? Why would I do that? I only needed the one.

And Vlad coming to my rescue. How did he get here in such a timely fashion?

Then I remember him talking about hypothetically watching my meeting with Sandra through the cameras.

I guess that wasn't hypothetical. He really does watch what happens here, at least when he's jealous.

Hanging up, Vlad turns his ferocious stare my way. "I knew something was off about this meeting."

I take a step back. "I thought he was Phantom. How was I—"

"Phantom?" He pronounces the word with a strong Russian accent. "He isn't. I am."

"You?"

I feel like a dope.

Of course it's him. That long conversation with my mom about opera. Elegant code. Concern about the privacy of my photo database.

Who else could it have been?

"Why didn't you just say so?" I ask dazedly.

My emotions are all over the place. I have no idea what to think about any of this.

He scrubs a hand over his face. "I wanted the freedom to mentor you without complicating our already-complex relationship. More importantly, it simply didn't come up."

Complex relationship.

That's an understatement of the century.

"How did they find out about the testing?" I sneak a peek at the office floor through the glass walls. "Sandra?"

His jaw muscles tense. "She wouldn't. I think you revealed it. Inadvertently."

"Me?" The question is the closest I can get to a growl. "What are you talking about?"

"You don't take privacy seriously." The words come out clipped—an accusation if there ever was one. "I guessed the password on your source control repository effortlessly. Chocula2019, right?"

I stagger back. "How?"

"The whimsical variable name you overused, plus the current year. Not rocket science. And I bet you use the same exact password to log into the cloud server where you keep the testing documentation. Tell me I'm wrong."

He's not wrong, but he also couldn't make me feel stupider if he tried.

I start to see red. "You hacked me?"

He gives me one of his Impaler glares. "Someone else hacked you. I cleaned up that counter variable, remember? I was looking out for you."

What bullshit. "If you knew my password wasn't secure, why didn't you tell me?"

"I didn't get a chance. Besides, I didn't want you to think I was invading your privacy."

"Right, okay. And now my reputation is in shambles." A situation made infinitely worse by the fact that it's all my fault.

I couldn't feel more embarrassed if I tried.

He sighs and adjusts his glasses. He looks infinitely less angry now. "I'll have to look into that rumor business. For now, you should change your passwords everywhere you can think of. Better late than never. Instead of using the letters in your favorite word, you can swap them for numbers that correspond to the position of those letters in the alphabet. Or just use—"

"Don't patronize me!" Rationally, I know I'm not being entirely fair, but I can't take this anymore. The cauldron of anger and embarrassment in my chest has reached its boiling point. "I aced a class in cryptography in the same school as you."

His eyebrows snap together. "I wasn't—"

"I'm leaving." I circle around him and head for the door.

"What about the lunch?" he calls to my back.

"I lost my appetite." I sprint for the elevators.

I'm not running away from him so much as this office, with its toxic rumors.

To my relief, no one crosses my path on the way. As soon as an elevator door opens, I jump inside and jab the lobby button.

As the doors are closing, I spot Vlad stalking toward me, his expression night dark.

He's chasing me?

Doesn't matter.

The elevator doors slide shut before he can jam his hand in.

———

In the cab on the way home, I replay what just happened in my head.

Over and over.

No matter which angle I look from, what used to be my great reputation at Binary Birch is now history.

Though people don't know that I went full cliché and actually slept with the company owner, they do think I used toys on him and on other dudes—the latter being a hurtful lie. No matter what happens now, the specter of preferential treatment will taint my career, which sucks because I work hard at my job. In fact, I got into this mess *because* I was such a good tester. Not that anyone will care anymore. Now they'll assume I'm using sex to get what I want, be it a transfer into the development department or a promotion.

The worst part is, if I do get that transfer now, I myself won't be sure it happened for the right reasons.

As the cab enters Brooklyn, my thoughts turn to Vlad, and my embarrassment and anger give way to a mix of guilt and regret.

I shouldn't have stormed out on him the way I did. What happened wasn't his fault.

I mean, could he—Mr. Privacy—have handled the password situation better?

Probably.

Did he owe me the Phantom info?

Not exactly.

In fact, Phantom's praise had actually felt nicer, more deserved *before* I knew Vlad was behind it.

We stop next to my place.

I pay and rush to my door.

A package is waiting for me there.

Inside the box is a fanny pack—though it calls itself "a waist bag." It's Chanel, stylish as hell, and contains a note signed by Vlad:

Own it.

I don't know how I should feel about this. The bag must cost thousands of dollars.

The shipping date is from the day before yesterday, so he didn't know about today's mess when he sent it. Or that we'd sleep together.

Is it a sign that he likes me or a thank-you for a testing job well done?

I know I'm not thinking clearly right now, so I take out Precious and call Ava.

She doesn't pick up.

I leave her a voicemail to call me back ASAP, and even send her an SOS text.

No reply.

Maybe I should email her for good measure? Sometimes she checks her inbox from her work computer when her phone is dead.

I launch my email, and something in my inbox catches my eye.

It's that Google alert I'd created to monitor for news mentioning Vlad's name.

Curious, I click on the alert and open the article in question.

It's on *Cosmopolitan*'s website. The tagline states:

Belka sex toys so addictive, reclusive CEO Vlad Chortsky couldn't help but test on himself.

Chapter Thirty

*P*recious slips out of my fingers, hitting the floor with a thud.

Hands shaking, I pick up my poor phone.

The screen is cracked, but the article is still visible and I'm able to read the rest of it.

According to a source, Vlad and a female QA tester couldn't help themselves and used the toys to reach multiple orgasms. The article even goes as far as to list the number of orgasms he and I had, and every type of toy used.

What's worse, they have a picture of Vlad, and I recognize it. It's the very same one I snapped at Starbucks when I first saw him, the one used by my app.

This proves it.

Vlad was right when he said that it was me and not Sandra who's responsible for this info getting out. Someone snooped around that public photo database my app uses—the very same one that Phantom/Vlad had suggested I make more private. The leaker dug out that photo and guessed my password to get my testing results from my documentation. They then handed all this to *Cosmo*, along with the gossip about Vlad, whose name wasn't in my write-up.

Since the *Cosmo* folks were going to write a story about Belka toys anyway, they jumped at the chance to make it juicier.

This would be bad even if Vlad weren't obsessed with privacy. As is, I can't even fathom how pissed he'll be when he learns about this.

Fuck.

Between my storming out earlier and this, I doubt I'll ever hear from him again.

Feeling masochistic, I text him the link to the article, asking, *Have you seen this?*

No reply.

I begin to pace my apartment.

With every second he doesn't text me back, I get more anxious.

He could at the very least say *something*, even if it's "You're fired" or "I never want to see you again."

To calm myself down, I grab some treats and go to feed Monkey.

She's not alone.

Of course.

Vlad left Oracle here.

That's just great. Every time a guy dumps my ass, I get another guinea pig.

Soon, I'll have a whole pigsty.

Since this isn't Oracle's fault, I feed both of them as they squeak and run around, popcorning in joy.

Their cute antics actually make me feel a little better. That is, until I get angry—but this time, not at Vlad.

It's the hacker.

The person who actually contacted *Cosmo*, and no doubt spread those rumors around the office as well.

Whoever it is, I hate them, and it's always good to know who you hate.

Jumping on my laptop, I navigate my way to my cloud storage account and check access history for the testing document.

It doesn't take long to locate what I'm looking for.

Someone who lives in Queens—as in, not me— has regularly accessed the file in the last couple of days.

I grit my teeth. The IP of the scum looks familiar.

I bring up the IP of that CrazyOops user who'd said catty things about my app.

Yep.

It's a match.

Which means there's a very good chance it was Britney behind all this.

Not a huge surprise. She's known as a hacker, she hates my guts, and she's been sniffing around this project from the start. She'd even stalked our lunches.

Vlad being rude to her at the monthly meeting probably didn't help matters.

Fuming, I go down the rabbit hole of internet

searches to find out if what she did is legal.

Nope. Unauthorized access to computer systems is a crime.

Speaking of crimes, smothering Britney would also not be legal, no matter how good it would feel.

I resume my pacing.

It's been hours now, and nothing from Vlad.

I might as well admit it.

He's ghosting me—and I can't blame him.

His privacy is kaput, all because of my negligence, and his sister didn't get the write-up she'd hoped for.

Well, screw him. By not talking to me, he's missing the Britney info.

This might actually be for the best. I was beginning to fall for that bastard, and if he's like this, I'd rather learn early.

Yeah. I should thank him for not texting.

This is like ripping off a Band-Aid.

That's always a good idea, right?

Maybe not if the Band-Aid is covering a festering wound.

I stop pacing and force myself to eat.

Everything tastes like cardboard. Montages of my lunches with Vlad play out in my treacherous brain, followed by recollections of us cuddling last night.

And the orgasms he gave me.

Okay, need major distraction.

I immerse myself in video games—something I haven't done in a while. It helps a bit. Beheading zombies isn't as satisfying as scalping Britney would be, but at least it's more socially acceptable.

Maybe this is what I should've done with my computer science degree: made games that let people forget the crap in their lives, at least for a while.

By midnight, any hope I had for a reply from Vlad is gone, so I stumble into bed and cry myself to sleep.

————

I wake up to the chime of a doorbell.

Leaping off the bed, I rush to the bathroom and make myself semi-presentable before sprinting for the door.

"Who is it?" I ask, then belatedly recall that I can now look at the video app on my phone.

"Ava."

Crap. I've never been so disappointed to hear my friend's voice.

I open the door.

She looks furious. "Who texts SOS and then ignores her friend's calls?"

I blink at her. "I didn't ignore you."

She pushes her way in. "I texted and called a hundred times. Literally."

"Hold up." I stumble into the living room and pick up Precious. "Nothing from you."

She scoffs. "I called and texted. Repeatedly."

A sinking feeling builds in my stomach—but also a flutter of hope.

I check Precious more thoroughly.

Damn it. It's not just the screen that's cracked. When I dropped it, it also lost the ability to receive calls and messages.

Which means Vlad might not have ghosted me.

I was too out of it yesterday to realize that Ava had also disappeared on me. If I were in my right mind, that would've raised all sorts of red flags.

Ava puts her hands on her hips. "You need to spill whatever it is. Now."

I make us two bowls of chocolatey cereal, and we gobble it down as I give her the whole awful story.

"I bet he thinks you ghosted *him*," Ava says. "You stormed out and all that."

I put down my spoon. "That's what I'm afraid of."

She slurps the last of her milk. "So what now?"

"Give me your phone."

She does. I pull up Vlad's number on my mostly dead Precious and call Vlad from Ava's phone.

He doesn't answer.

Maybe he's screening numbers he doesn't know?

I look for my work phone but can't find it.

Did I forget it at his place, just like my panties?

No. It must've been that meeting room.

I remember putting it down on the table, but I have zero recollection of picking it up.

Fuck it.

I jump to my feet. "I'm going to go to him."

Ava wrinkles her nose. "You might want to make yourself look like a human first."

"Right." I drop our bowls into the sink. "I'm sorry

you came all this way just to watch me leave."

She grins. "Don't worry about me. It might be fun to help you get ready."

I rush into my closet and look for something to wear that screams "grand romantic gesture."

It doesn't take me long to pick out the perfect thing.

It's my Halloween costume of many years in a row.

Donning the black vinyl, I return to the living room.

"What do you know?" Ava says, scanning me from head to toe. "Yet another rich guy into BDSM."

I roll my eyes. "I'm supposed to be Trinity from *The Matrix*, and you know it."

She grins. "Let me help you with makeup."

"How about you do it on the way?"

She agrees, and I get her to order us an Uber.

While we wait for the car, I check my work email, just in case.

As I suspected, there are countless messages from Vlad, proving without a shadow of a doubt that he didn't ghost me.

You're not answering your phone, one says. *Can we talk?*

Next one: *I understand why you're upset. Can you call me?*

I scroll down to the fifteenth email.

Just found your work phone. Did you lose your personal one as well?

Before I read any more, Ava's phone informs us

that the driver is outside. We run out and jump into the car, where Ava makes me look borderline goth—a makeup style that works nicely with my dark hair and pale skin tone.

"Go get him," she says when the car stops next to my work building. "You look amazeballs."

"Thanks." I jump out and put on my Matrix-inspired sunshades before rushing into the building.

Exiting the elevator on the Binary Birch floor, I bump right into a bunch of people with coffees in their hands. They're exiting the other elevator.

Ugh. They're from the dev team, and thanks to Murphy's law, Britney is among them.

I suppress the urge to go for her throat. Murder is wrong, and downright dumb when you're surrounded by so many witnesses.

Clearly unaware of the danger she's in, Britney looks me over with an eye roll. "Is it time to test the nipple clamps already?"

The people around us shift their gazes between us, looking uncomfortable.

I take off my shades so I can properly glare at her. "Your jokes are as crap as your coding skills."

A few bystander eyebrows shoot up.

She narrows her eyes at me. "What could you possibly know about coding, you hack?"

Red mist veils my vision. I've been waiting for this for so, so long. "More than you, that's for sure. You don't use consistent indentation, you leave zero comments, and you misspell the words in variable names half the time. And I don't think you even know the meaning of 'modularization.' Do I need to keep going? Because I can."

To my shock, several of her teammates nod approvingly. Someone even mutters something like, "Mad burn."

Britney squeezes her coffee so hard it spills over. "At least I didn't let the Impaler poke me with a dildo."

My glare can melt lead at this point. "He wouldn't poke *you* with a ten-foot pole, that's for sure."

She bristles, advancing on me. "How dare you?"

Fine. No more Ms. Nice Fanny. "I know it was you," I grit through my teeth.

Blanching, she stops in her tracks. "I don't know what you're talking about."

I rattle out her IP address. "Does that sound familiar? Because I called your ISP, and they confirmed that's yours."

I did no such thing, but the bluff clearly works. She whitens to ghost levels and takes a step back.

Time for the kill—unfortunately metaphorical. "If I see your face or IP address ever again, I'm going to give the info to the Impaler. Given how crazy he is about privacy, and how rich, he'll probably make sure you rot in jail."

She's so green I'm tempted to give her Dramamine. "It was just a joke."

I put my sunglasses back on. "Like I said, your jokes are as crap as your code."

Chapter Thirty-One

*N*ot waiting to see the dev team's reaction, I hurry down the hallway and barge into Vlad's office.

He's not here.

Damn it.

Where is he?

I look for a calendar, but of course, this isn't 1989 or whenever it was when everyone stopped using paper.

Bolstered by my outfit and the encounter with Britney, I circle around Vlad's desk and wake up his computer.

It's locked.

Of course. Standard company policy—which sucks, because if I could sneak a peek at his digital calendar, I'd figure out where he is.

If only I could guess his pin code…

I bite my lip, considering it.

Our pin codes are six digits, so there are a million different random combinations.

So guessing at random is out.

I have to try to think of what he might actually use.

I look up, and sure enough, there's a security camera in the corner of his office.

Is that in case someone tries what I'm about to do?

Well, hopefully he won't be too mad at me.

I wave at the camera. "This is what you get for stalking me in your meeting rooms."

Just in case he watches the tape later.

For now, I try 123456 for the pin code.

Nope. That would've been too easy.

I try 654321.

Still no.

I try different permutations of his birth date.

None work.

The beginning and end digits of his phone number don't work either.

If I keep this up, the computer will lock me out for too many failed attempts.

Then I recall something he'd said right before I stormed out of that meeting room, about how you can use numbers to represent the letters of the alphabet in a favorite word.

Could it be that simple?

I convert what I think might be his favorite word —Neo—to 140515.

Score!

The computer unlocks, and the first thing that stares me in the face is an email Vlad must've been drafting before he locked his screen.

Its subject line states: "Britney Archibald's Termination."

Unable to help myself, I skim the message.

Of course.

Vlad figured out she was the leak and the one spreading the rumors. Attached are transcripts of instant messenger conversations where she told Mike how I was testing sex toys with multiple men at Binary Birch, including the guy in HR whose name happens to be in the "To" of Vlad's email.

She is so screwed.

Somehow, Vlad even managed to dig up proof that Britney had hacked the social media accounts of her ex from the sales department—something that was only rumored until now.

It's official.

Britney bit off more than she could chew when she gave Vlad's name to *Cosmo*.

Minimizing the email, I check Vlad's calendar to see where he is.

Huh.

He's at 1000 Devils, and where the agenda should be is my name.

Is he asking his brother for some relationship advice?

That doesn't track. Vlad has attached my resume

to this meeting, as well as links to my app's code. I'd hope those aren't critical for any relationship we might or might not have.

Then it hits me.

He's getting me a job.

Leaping out of his chair, I sprint out of the building and jump into a cab.

Time to face 1000 Devils.

Chapter Thirty-Two

I step out of the elevator furtively.

Nope.

No one shoots me.

At least not yet.

Sprinting for the Nerf gun armory, I get myself a proper arsenal: two handguns that I stuff into my waistband and a two-handed machine-gun contraption.

If I'm going to work at this place—and I don't know if I am—I'll have to fit in with their quirky culture.

If that means shooting my way to Vlad, so be it.

Clutching my Nerf machine gun, I exit the room and creep onto the main floor.

An orange projectile is hurtling at my face, but I sidestep and it whooshes by my ear.

"Nice one," someone says.

I spin around and put a bullet in the chest of a

redhead with a beer belly. I vaguely remember him from my last visit.

Someone jumps out of the cube on the right.

I dodge her shot, then shoot her in the boob.

Another person leaps out of a cube.

I lunge behind a column, avoiding the projectile.

Peeking out to take aim, I kneecap the last assailant.

A bunch of darts hits the column.

I stick my head out, spot an older lady unloading her gun in my direction, and shoot her in the arm.

Another round of darts misses me.

I peek once more.

A guy with a buzzcut is reloading.

I shoot his neck, then sprint for the column near the large meeting room.

Through the glass, I see Vlad and Alex speaking animatedly, but they don't notice me.

Which is fine.

I don't need backup anyway.

Taking in a deep breath, I sprint out of my hiding spot.

The next few moments happen like a slow-motion effect in *The Matrix*.

I dodge a dart, then hit its source in the shoulder.

Leaping over a low-flying projectile, I drop my empty machine gun to the floor and pull out two handguns while still in the air.

Bang. Bang.

Two handed, I hit two people in my path to the meeting room and grab the door handle.

A whole cloud of Nerf darts is now flying my way, but I'm already behind the glass door.

The darts hit the glass and drop futilely to the floor.

Victory!

"Fanny?" Vlad is staring at me with a mixture of confusion and approval. "What are you doing here? How did you get here?"

I take off my sunglasses. "Guessed your pin code and took a peek at your calendar. Sorry about before. My phone was broken. I wasn't ignoring you. Because of the article, I thought—" I stop, catching the fascinated expression on Alex's face. "Never mind."

A slow smile spreads over Vlad's face. "It's good that you came. We were just talking about you."

Alex stands up. "Hey there, Fanny. Good to see you again." He shakes my hand. "I was going to get my HR folks to reach out to you first, but since you're here, I want to formally extend you an offer for a developer position here at 1000 Devils."

So, my guess was correct.

Vlad is getting me another job.

And not just any job.

Software development, exactly what I want to do.

My excitement battles with embarrassment. Before this goes any further, I have to ask Alex something important. "Is this because I slept with your brother?"

Eyes widening, Alex darts Vlad a questioning glance. "You did? I guess… good for you guys?"

If I hoped that recent events had desensitized my cheeks from burning, no such luck. They heat up with an almost sadistic enthusiasm as I sneak a peek at Vlad.

Did I just blurt something I shouldn't have?

Will he be even madder at me now?

His face is unreadable, though one corner of his mouth appears to be twitching in either amusement or anger.

Alex scratches the back of his head. "Actually, Fanny, I wanted to hire you after you found that glitch in our game, but Vlad and I have a no-poaching policy, so I figured it wasn't meant to be. When he told me you're looking for something more fun and challenging, but in the coding area instead of testing, I got intrigued. And since he just showed me your recent work, I have no doubt you'd be an asset here. We're currently working on an RPG where we want to match user's images to a database of pre-prepared character faces that look like them. Does that sound familiar?"

My excitement grows with each word he speaks, and by the time he's done, I can't help but bob my head repeatedly. "That's basically what my app does." My voice all but bursts with eagerness. "Just replace cartoon characters with game ones."

Alex smiles. "Exactly. You'll be able to hit the ground running. Assuming you're interested?" His expression turns more serious. "Before you decide, I can tell you here and now: Whatever happens between you and my brother will never have any bearing on your job. I can put that in legalese if you want me to."

I grin so widely I can feel it in my ears. "In that case, yes."

I extend my hand, and we shake on it.

Vlad rises to his feet. "She actually means 'maybe.' To get a yes, you need to wow her with things like salary and benefits."

I almost smack myself on the forehead. "Vlad's right. My talents don't come cheap."

Alex grins. "I'm sure we can work something out. It's Binary Birch we're competing with, after all." He gives Vlad a good-natured wink. "For example, our dress code is less restrictive—Matrix attire being purely optional."

I beam at him. "Thank you. This is very exciting. I'll be on the lookout for a formal offer. Now if you don't mind, I need to talk to Vlad." I give my-soon-to-be former employer a hesitant smile. "Assuming you *want* to talk to me?"

Vlad cocks his head. "We can talk… provided you let me cook you a lunch of my choice."

I resist the urge to jump up and down like a kid. "It's a deal."

As Alex walks us out of the 1000 Devils building, I make the easiest decision of my life.

Unless it's a huge pay cut—and I doubt that very

much—I'll take the 1000 Devils' job. Making video games is something every gamer thinks about as soon as they start their introductory programming classes, and a company like this seems particularly cool. The culture at 1000 Devils is quirky, with the guns and all —but that just seems like a fun adventure, not a drawback.

In fact, even if I'm given the option to work from home, I'll work here at the office.

"I missed you," Vlad says when the elevator doors close.

I snap to attention, all thoughts of the job offer forgotten. "I missed you too," I say, proud of how steady my voice is. "I'm sorry about—"

"No." He takes my hand, his fingers strong and warm around mine. "I'm the one who should be sorry. I should've fired Britney after she hacked that guy in sales. You heard about that, right?"

Oops. I guess hacking is on his list of no-nos. "Did you hear me earlier? I got into your computer. And when I did, I saw the email you were writing about her. I'm sorry about invading your privacy like that."

He squeezes my hand reassuringly. "I guessed your password, and you guessed my pin. I'd say we're even."

I want to kiss him, but the elevator opens and people look at us expectantly, so we get out.

The walk to the limo happens in a flash, with me feeling like I'm waltzing on air the whole time. Climbing in, we sit next to each other, and he buckles my safety belt as though that's a normal thing to do—and I love it.

"How did your sister take the whole article debacle?" I ask when the car rushes forward.

He smiles. "Her phone is off the hook. She thinks the hint of scandal in the article actually helped. She might be right. The original would've sounded more like an infomercial."

Whew. "So she's going to be okay?"

His smile widens. "Yep."

I bite my lip. "How about you?"

"All good as well. I contacted *Cosmo* with a correction to the article, and they fixed it." He pulls out his phone and shows me the screen.

I skim the article. His name is still there, but I'm no longer referred to as a QA person.

According to this article, I'm Vlad's girlfriend.

Girlfriend.

Me.

I want to jump out of the car and dance a jig in the middle of Times Square.

"That's okay, right?" he asks, his dark brows furrowing. "I figured that—"

"It's more than okay." The words come out breathlessly. "But why didn't you make them remove your name from the article while you were at it?"

He shrugs. "Didn't want to risk it. What if the correction reduces the exposure for Bella?"

I nod solemnly. "Very noble. Sacrificing your privacy for your sister."

A corner of his mouth twists wryly. "That, or I don't have that much leverage over the folks at *Cosmo*."

The limo stops, and he opens the door for me.

As we get into his building, he tells me about a guinea pig herd he discovered upstate—a place where owners can let their pets play with large numbers of other piggies.

"Monkey and Oracle looked like they enjoyed being together," he explains as we ride the elevator. "So I started to wonder whether they wouldn't want even more socialization."

"Sure," I say as the elevator opens into his place. "I like the idea of this herd. We'll take them there one day."

The part I like the most is that he's making plans that involve me.

First, I'm his girlfriend, and now this.

The only way I'd feel happier is if he got naked.

Hmm. Maybe this can also be arranged?

"So…" I take off my boots. "You never gave me a tour of your place."

He hands me a pair of slippers that happen to be exactly my size—making me feel like Cinderella.

"I'm going to fix that oversight immediately." He opens the door down the hall. "This is my bedroom."

Check and mate. Bedroom is the destination I needed for my evil plan.

Once we're inside, I close the door loudly to get his attention. Then, as he watches, I unzip my top.

Dracula displays immediate interest—as does Vlad.

His eyes gleam predatorially behind his lenses as he closes the distance between us. "That outfit has been driving me insane."

I reach over to unbutton his shirt collar. "Right back at ya."

"Wait." He catches my wrists. "There's something you should know."

"Oh?" A kaleidoscope of butterflies flaps their wings together, starting a whirlwind in my belly.

He takes a breath, his expression uncertain for the first time since I've known him. Softly, he says, "It's going to sound crazy, but I've never experienced this kind of connection with anyone before. The way we are together is like the most elegant, bug-free code that works perfectly as soon as you finish writing it. Fannychka…" His voice roughens. "I know it's only been a few days since we met, but—"

"You love me," I blurt—and flush immediately.

I have no idea where this bold statement came from, but I'm absurdly certain I'm right.

He lets go of my wrists, amusement glinting in his eyes. "Is it some American custom to interrupt such things?"

My already-prodigious blush deepens. "I'm so sorry. You were saying?"

He takes my face into his hands, the way he did the other day when he told me he'd like me even without any facial hair. His eyes are the purest, deepest blue as they peer into mine. "Fanny Pack," he says solemnly. "I love you."

The storm in my belly morphs into a full-fledged tornado, one that spins higher up my chest, encasing my heart with the warmest, sweetest glow. "And I love you," I breathe.

He leans in, claiming my lips in the deepest, most passionate kiss. Lips locked and tongues dancing, we stumble to the bed, our clothes falling off as if by magic, and what happens next can only be described by one word.

Lovemaking.

Hours later, as we lie there utterly spent, I secretly pinch myself to make sure this is really happening.

It is.

It's real.

I've gotten the vampire of my dreams, Vlad the Impaler himself.

Who could've guessed?

And just to think… it all started with a suitcase full of sex toys.

Epilogue

Six months later, Iceland

n our table is a plate of peculiar Icelandic delicacies, including fermented shark and soured ram testicles.

I'm not surprised that Fannychka has bravely tried a bite of every single thing here and liked it, even the poor ram's nads—a dish I personally skipped. Out of, as she teasingly put it, "male solidarity."

In the last six months, she's become a connoisseur of delicacies from all around the globe—at least, the ones you can get in NYC, which is many.

She's also a connoisseur of sexual acts, positions, and toys, much to my delight. If she ever gets tired of being a game developer, I bet she could write the next Kama Sutra.

This is our first official vacation, and she's loved it thus far—though more thanks to the geothermal pools and the alien-planet landscapes rather than the Icelandic cuisine.

I keep my face neutral as I watch her drink her apple cider, though the sight of those scrumptious pink lips wrapped around the bottle drives me insane, as usual.

Does she have any clue what I'm about to do?

Maybe. Maybe not. You never know with this one. She can be deviously clever.

I scan our surroundings for clues.

The glass roof and walls of the restaurant create an uber-romantic ambience that could give me away. You can see city lights down the mountain, as well as the night sky above.

Also, we're the only ones here, so she might right-fully deduce this is my doing and not the restaurant suffering from a lack of patrons.

Hopefully, the not-so-romantic food selection was a good-enough misdirection.

Now I just need the weather to cooperate. The forecast was good, but if not, there's always tomorrow.

I want her to remember this forever.

So, I carry on a conversation as we eat, but I also wait for my moment.

As par for the course on such auspicious occasions, I can't help but think back on some of the highlights of our time together.

When I saw her at that Starbucks, with her pale skin and black hair, she'd looked like she stepped out of the *Underworld* movies—ironic, considering all the vampire jokes she still makes at my expense.

I knew then and there that I wanted her, and I took a picture of her surreptitiously—another bit of irony considering she did the same to me with her app.

When she stepped into my office mere minutes later, she looked like I might eat her—cannibalistically —while the truth was that I wanted to devour her in a very different way, completely inappropriate for the office.

I tried to stay professional—not an easy task given the project on her plate—but then she contacted me with that toy emergency, and all my good intentions went out the window. I was shocked at the protective emotions she stirred up. A part of me knew most people would find her situation humorous, but I was way too worried about her getting hurt.

Things began to spiral even more when I took her to our first lunch and started to learn how much we had in common. By the time she told me she wanted to test the toys on some random guy, I wanted to rip him into shreds.

Then the testing started.

Dracula gets rock hard every time I think about that—including now. It's a good thing I don't need to get up anytime soon, else—

"Look, babe, the Northern Lights!" Fanny is

gesturing at the glass roof, her blue eyes shining in excitement.

Spoke too soon. I do have to move, erection or not.

This is the moment I've been waiting for.

Fanny has been dying to see this wonder, and I can't blame her. As a kid, I couldn't get enough of watching these things back in Murmansk.

It's a perfect distraction, so I ignore the bulge in my pants along with the gorgeous aurora borealis in the sky.

By the time she looks back at me, I'm in position.

On one knee, a diamond ring in hand.

A ring my sister and Ava helped me choose—before I swore them to secrecy, of course.

"Fuck. Me." Fanny gapes down at me, her pupils the size of a dime. "When did you get down there?"

Seems like she didn't expect this.

Good.

Ignoring the question, I launch into my spiel. "Fanny Pack, I first want to thank you for all the joy you've brought into my life." I know that sounds like one of my parents' toasts, but the words are coming from my heart, and the bright glitter of her eyes seems to indicate that they resonate. "You have been the most important thing in my world for the last six months. I love you, and you love me. Will you—"

"Marry you?" she breathes.

I grin. It's become a tradition of sorts for her to

interrupt me during moments like this; she did it even when I asked her to move in together.

I lovingly clasp her small hand. "I was actually going to say: Will you make me the happiest vampire in history by letting me finally turn you, so we can spend an eternity together?"

She spreads the fingers on her free hand. "Yes. Please. I've always wanted to sparkle in the sunlight."

Heart thudding heavily in my chest, I slide the ring on her finger, making it official.

Our big adventure together is about to begin.

Acknowledgments

Thank you for participating in Vlad and Fanny's journey! If you enjoyed it, please consider leaving a review. Can't get enough of the Chortsky family? Read Bella's story in *Hard Ware*, and Alex's story in *Hard Byte*! And be sure to check out *Royally Tricked*, a feel-good romcom starring daredevil Tigger (from *Hard Ware)* and Gia, the twin sister of Holly from *Hard Byte*.

Misha Bell is a collaboration between husband-and-wife writing team, Dima Zales and Anna Zaires. When they're not making you bust a gut as Misha, Dima writes sci-fi and fantasy, and Anna writes dark and contemporary romance. If you loved *Hard Code*'s humor and found yourself wishing Vlad turned out to be a real vampire, check out the *Sasha Urban* series by Dima Zales. If you want more steamy hotness, especially with a possessive alpha billionaire, check out *Wall Street Titan* by Anna Zaires. Turn the page to read previews of both!

Excerpt from Wall Street Titan

A billionaire who wants a perfect wife...

At thirty-five, Marcus Carelli has it all: wealth, power, and the kind of looks that leave women breathless. A self-made billionaire, he heads one of the largest hedge funds on Wall Street and can take down major corporations with a single word. The only thing he's missing? A wife who'd be as big of an achievement as the billions in his bank account.

A cat lady who needs a date...

Twenty-six-year-old bookstore clerk Emma Walsh has it on good authority that she's a cat lady. She doesn't necessarily agree with that assessment, but it's hard to argue with the facts. Raggedy clothes covered with cat hair? Check. Last professional haircut? Over a year ago. Oh, and three cats in a tiny Brooklyn studio? Yep, she's got those.

And yes, fine, she hasn't had a date since… well, she can't recall. But that part is fixable. Isn't that what the dating sites are for?

A case of mistaken identity…

One high-end matchmaker, one dating app, one mix-up that changes everything... Opposites may attract, but can this last?

————

I'm all but bouncing with excitement as I approach Sweet Rush Café, where I'm supposed to meet Mark for dinner. This is the craziest thing I've done in a while. Between my evening shift at the bookstore and his class schedule, we haven't had a chance to do more than exchange a few text messages, so all I have to go on are those couple of blurry pictures. Still, I have a good feeling about this.

I feel like Mark and I might really connect.

I'm a few minutes early, so I stop by the door and take a moment to brush cat hair off my woolen coat. The coat is beige, which is better than black, but white hair is visible on anything that's not pure white. I figure Mark won't mind too much—he knows how much Persians shed—but I still want to look presentable for our first date. It took me about an hour, but I got my curls to semi-behave, and I'm even wearing a little makeup—something that happens with the frequency of a tsunami in a lake.

Taking a deep breath, I enter the café and look around to see if Mark might already be there.

The place is small and cozy, with booth-style seats arranged in a semicircle around a coffee bar. The smell of roasted coffee beans and baked goods is mouthwatering, making my stomach rumble with hunger. I was planning to stick to coffee only, but I decide to get a croissant too; my budget should stretch to that.

Only a few of the booths are occupied, likely because it's a Tuesday. I scan them, looking for anyone who could be Mark, and notice a man sitting by himself at the farthest table. He's facing away from me, so all I can see is the back of his head, but his hair is short and dark brown.

It could be him.

Gathering my courage, I approach the booth. "Excuse me," I say. "Are you Mark?"

The man turns to face me, and my pulse shoots into the stratosphere.

The person in front of me is nothing like the pictures on the app. His hair is brown, and his eyes are blue, but that's the only similarity. There's nothing rounded and shy about the man's hard features. From the steely jaw to the hawk-like nose, his face is boldly masculine, stamped with a self-assurance that borders on arrogance. A hint of five o'clock shadow darkens his lean cheeks, making his high cheekbones stand out even more, and his eyebrows are thick dark slashes above his piercingly pale eyes. Even sitting behind the table, he looks tall and powerfully built. His shoulders are a mile wide in his sharply tailored suit, and his hands are twice the size of my own.

There's no way this is Mark from the app, unless he's put in some serious gym time since those pictures were taken. Is it possible? Could a person change so much? He didn't indicate his height in the profile, but I'd assumed the omission meant he was vertically challenged, like me.

The man I'm looking at is not challenged in any way, and he's certainly not wearing glasses.

"I'm… I'm Emma," I stutter as the man continues staring at me, his face hard and inscrutable. I'm almost certain I have the wrong guy, but I still force myself to ask, "Are you Mark, by any chance?"

"I prefer to be called Marcus," he shocks me by answering. His voice is a deep masculine rumble that tugs at something primitively female inside me. My heart beats even faster, and my palms begin to sweat as he rises to his feet and says bluntly, "You're not what I expected."

"Me?" *What the hell?* A surge of anger crowds out all other emotions as I gape at the rude giant in front of me. The asshole is so tall I have to crane my neck to look up at him. "What about you? You look nothing like your pictures!"

"I guess we've both been misled," he says, his jaw tight. Before I can respond, he gestures toward the booth. "You might as well sit down and have a meal with me, Emmeline. I didn't come all the way here for nothing."

"It's *Emma*," I correct, fuming. "And no, thank you. I'll just be on my way."

His nostrils flare, and he steps to the right to block my path. "Sit down, *Emma*." He makes my name sound like an insult. "I'll have a talk with Victoria, but for now, I don't see why we can't share a meal like two civilized adults."

The tips of my ears burn with fury, but I slide into the booth rather than make a scene. My grandmother instilled politeness in me from an early age, and even as an adult living on my own, I find it hard to go against her teachings.

She wouldn't approve of me kneeing this jerk in the balls and telling him to fuck off.

"Thank you," he says, sliding into the seat across from me. His eyes glint icy blue as he picks up the menu. "That wasn't so hard, was it?"

"I don't know, *Marcus*," I say, putting special emphasis on the formal name. "I've only been around you for two minutes, and I'm already feeling homicidal." I deliver the insult with a ladylike, Grandma-approved smile, and dumping my purse in the corner of my booth seat, I pick up the menu without bothering to take off my coat.

The sooner we eat, the sooner I can get out of here.

A deep chuckle startles me into looking up. To my shock, the jerk is grinning, his teeth flashing white in his lightly bronzed face. No freckles for him, I note with jealousy; his skin is perfectly even-toned, without so much as an extra mole on his cheek. He's not classically handsome—his features are too bold to be described that way—but he's shockingly good-looking, in a potent, purely masculine way.

To my dismay, a curl of heat licks at my core, making my inner muscles clench.

No. No way. This asshole is *not* turning me on. I can barely stand to sit across the table from him.

Gritting my teeth, I look down at my menu, noting with relief that the prices in this place are actually reasonable. I always insist on paying for my own food on dates, and now that I've met Mark—excuse me, *Marcus*—I wouldn't put it past him to drag me to some ritzy place where a glass of tap water costs more than a shot of Patrón. How could I have been so wrong about the guy? Clearly, he'd lied about working in a bookstore and being a student. To what end, I don't know, but everything about the man in front of me screams wealth and power. His pinstriped suit hugs his broad-shouldered frame like it was tailor-made for him, his blue shirt is crisply starched, and I'm pretty sure his subtly checkered tie is some designer brand that makes Chanel seem like a Walmart label.

As all of these details register, a new suspicion occurs to me. Could someone be playing a joke on me? Kendall, perhaps? Or Janie? They both know my taste in guys. Maybe one of them decided to lure me on a date this way—though why they'd set me up with *him*, and he'd agree to it, is a huge mystery.

Frowning, I look up from the menu and study the man in front of me. He's stopped grinning and is perusing the menu, his forehead creased in a frown that makes him look older than the twenty-seven years listed on his profile.

That part must've also been a lie.

My anger intensifies. "So, *Marcus*, why did you write to me?" Dropping the menu on the table, I glare at him. "Do you even own cats?"

He looks up, his frown deepening. "Cats? No, of course not."

The derision in his tone makes me want to forget all about Grandma's disapproval and slap him straight across his lean, hard face. "Is this some kind of a prank for you? Who put you up to this?"

"Excuse me?" His thick eyebrows rise in an arrogant arch.

"Oh, stop playing innocent. You lied in your message to me, and you have the gall to say *I'm* not what you expected?" I can practically feel the steam coming out of my ears. "*You* messaged *me*, and I was entirely truthful on my profile. How old are you? Thirty-two? Thirty-three?"

"I'm thirty-five," he says slowly, his frown returning. "Emma, what are you talking——"

"That's it." Grabbing my purse by one strap, I slide out of the booth and jump to my feet. Grandma's teachings or not, I'm not going to have a meal with a jerk who's admitted to deceiving me. I have no idea what would make a guy like that want to toy with me, but I'm not going to be the butt of some joke.

"Enjoy your meal," I snarl, spinning around, and stride to the exit before he can block my way again.

I'm in such a rush to leave I almost knock over a tall, slender brunette approaching the café and the short, pudgy guy following her.

––––––––

Order your copy of *Wall Street Titan* today at
www.annazaires.com!

Excerpt from The Girl Who Sees by Dima Zales

I'm an illusionist, not a psychic.

Going on TV is supposed to advance my career, but things go wrong.

Like vampires and zombies kind of wrong.

My name is Sasha Urban, and this is how I learned what I am.

————

"I'm not a psychic," I say to the makeup girl. "What I'm about to do is mentalism."

"Like that dreamy guy on the TV show?" The makeup girl adds another dash of foundation to my cheekbones. "I always wanted to do his makeup. Can you also hypnotize and read people?"

I take a deep, calming breath. It doesn't help much. The tiny dressing room smells like hairspray went to war with nail polish remover, won, and took some fumes prisoner.

"Not exactly," I say when I have my anxiety and subsequent irritation under control. Even with Valium in my blood, the knowledge of what's about to come keeps me on the edge of sanity. "A mentalist is a type of stage magician whose illusions deal with the mind. If it were up to me, I'd just go by 'mental illusionist.'"

"That's not a very good name." She blinds me with her lamp and carefully examines my eyebrows.

I mentally cringe; the last time she looked at me this way, I ended up getting tortured with tweezers.

She must like what she sees now, though, because she turns the light away from my face. "'Mental illusionist' sounds like a psychotic magician," she continues.

"That's why I simply call myself an illusionist." I smile and prepare for the makeup to fall off, like a mask, but it stays put. "Are you almost done?"

"Let's see," she says, waving over a camera guy.

The guy makes me stand up, and the lights on his camera come on.

"This is it." The makeup girl points at the nearby LCD screen, where I have avoided looking until now because it's playing the ongoing show—the source of my panic.

The camera guy does whatever he needs to do,

and the anxiety-inducing show is gone from the screen, replaced by an image of our tiny room.

The girl on the screen vaguely resembles me. The heels make my usual five feet, six inches seem much taller, as does the dark leather outfit I'm wearing. Without heavy makeup, my face is symmetric enough, but my sharp cheekbones put me closer to handsome than pretty—an effect my strong chin enhances. The makeup, however, softens my features, bringing out the blue color of my eyes and highlighting the contrast with my black hair.

The makeup girl went overboard with it—you'd think I'm about to step into a shampoo commercial. I'm not a big fan of long hair, but I keep it that way because when I had it short, people used to mistake me for a teenage boy.

That's a mistake no one would make tonight.

"I like it," I say. "Let's be done. Please."

The TV guy switches the screen back to the live feed of the show. I can't help but glance there, and my already high blood pressure spikes.

The makeup girl looks me up and down and wrinkles her nose minutely. "You insist on that outfit, right?"

The really cool (in my opinion) borderline-dominatrix getup I've donned today is a means to add mystique to my onstage persona. Jean Eugène Robert-Houdin, the famous nineteenth-century French conjuror who inspired Houdini's stage name, once said, "A magician is an actor playing the part of a magician." When I saw Criss Angel on TV, back in elementary school, my opinion of what a magician should look like was formed, and I'm not too proud to admit that I see influences of his goth rock star look in my own outfit, especially the leather jacket.

"How marvelous," says a familiar voice with a sexy British accent. "You didn't look like this at the restaurant."

Pivoting on my high heels, I come face to face with Darian, the man I met two weeks ago at the restaurant where I do table-to-table magic—and where I'd impressed him enough to make this unimaginable opportunity a reality.

A senior producer on the popular *Evening with Kacie* show, Darian Rutledge is a lean, sharply dressed man who reminds me of a hybrid between a butler and James Bond. Despite his senior role at the studio and the frown lines that crisscross his forehead, I'd estimate his age to be late twenties—though that could be wishful thinking, given that I'm only twenty-four. Not that he's traditionally handsome or anything, but he does have a certain appeal. For one thing, with his strong nose, he's the rare guy who can pull off a goatee.

"I wear Doc Martens at the restaurant," I tell him. The extra inches of my footwear lift me to his eye level, and I can't help but get lost in those green depths. "The makeup was forced on me," I finish awkwardly.

He smiles and hands me a glass he's been holding.

"And the result is lovely. Cheers." He then looks at the makeup girl and the camera guy. "I'd like to speak with Sasha in private." His tone is polite, yet it carries an unmistakable air of imperiousness.

The staff bolt out of the room. Darian must be an even bigger shot than I thought.

On autopilot, I take a gulp of the drink he handed to me and wince at the bitterness.

"That's a Sea Breeze." He gives me a megaton smile. "The barman must've gone heavy on the grapefruit juice."

I take a polite second sip and put the drink on the vanity behind me, worried that the combination of vodka and Valium might make me woozier than I already am. I have no idea why Darian wants to speak to me alone; anxiety has already turned my brain to mush.

Darian regards me in silence for a moment, then pulls out a phone from his tight jeans' pocket. "There's a bit of unpleasantness we must discuss," he says, swiping across the screen of the phone before handing it to me.

I take the phone from him, gripping it tight so it doesn't slip out of my sweaty palms.

On the phone is a video.

I watch it in stunned silence, a wave of dread washing over me despite the medication.

The video reveals my secret—the hidden method behind the impossible feat I'm about to perform on *Evening with Kacie.*

I'm so screwed.

"Why are you showing me this?" I manage to say after I regain control of my paralyzed vocal cords.

Darian gently takes the phone back from my shaking hands. "You know that thing you went on about at the restaurant? How you're just pretending to be a psychic and that it's all tricks?"

"Right." I frown in confusion. "I never said I do anything for real. If this is about exposing me as a fraud—"

"You misunderstand." Darian grabs my discarded drink and takes a long, yet somehow elegant sip. "I have no intention of showing that video to anyone. Quite the contrary."

I blink at him, my brain clearly overheated from the adrenaline and lack of sleep.

"I know that as a magician, you don't like your methods known." His smile turns oddly predatory.

"Right," I say, wondering if he's about to make a blackmail-style indecent proposal. If he did, I would reject it, of course—but on principle, not because doing something indecent with a guy like Darian is unthinkable.

When you haven't gotten any for as long as I haven't, all sorts of crazy scenarios swirl through your head on a regular basis.

Darian's green gaze turns distant, as though he's trying to look through the nearby wall all the way into the horizon. "I know what you're planning on saying after the big reveal," he says, focusing back on me. In an eerie parody of my voice, he enunciates, "'I'm not a prophet. I use my five senses, principles of deception, and showmanship to create the illusion of being one.'"

My eyebrows rise so high my heavy makeup is in danger of chipping. He didn't approximate what I was about to say—he nailed it word for word, even copying the intonation I've practiced.

"Oh, don't look so surprised." He places the now-empty glass back on the vanity dresser. "You said that exact thing at the restaurant."

I nod, still in shock. Did I actually tell him this before? I don't remember, but I must have. Otherwise, how would he know?

"I paraphrased something another mentalist says," I blurt out. "Is this about giving him credit?"

"Not at all," Darian says. "I simply want you to omit that nonsense."

"Oh." I stare at him. "Why?"

Darian leans against the vanity and crosses his legs at the ankles. "What fun is it to have a fake psychic on the show? Nobody wants to see a fake."

"So you want me to act like a fraud? Pretend to be for real?" Between the stage fright, the video, and now this unreasonable demand, I'm just about ready to turn tail and run, even if I end up regretting it for the rest of my life.

He must sense that I'm about to lose it, because the predatory edge leaves his smile. "No, Sasha." His tone is exaggeratedly patient, as though he's talking to a small child. "I just want you to not say anything. Don't claim to be a psychic, but don't deny it either. Just avoid that topic altogether. Surely you can be comfortable with that."

"And if I'm not, you would show people the video? Reveal my method?"

The very idea outrages me. I might not want people to think I'm a psychic, but like most magicians, I work hard on the secret methods for my illusions, and I intend to take them to my grave—or write a book for magicians only, to be published posthumously.

"I'm sure it wouldn't come to that." Darian takes a step toward me, and the bergamot scent of his cologne teases my flaring nostrils. "We want the same thing, you and I. We want people to be enthralled by you. Just don't make any claims one way or another—that's all I ask."

I take a step back, his proximity too much for my already shaky state of mind. "Fine. You have a deal." I swallow thickly. "You never show the video, and I don't make any claims."

"There's one more thing, actually," he says, and I wonder if the indecent proposal is about to drop.

"What?" I dampen my lips nervously, then notice him looking and realize I'm just making an inappropriate pass at me that much more likely.

"How did you know what card my escort was thinking of?" he asks.

I smile, finally back in my element. He must be

talking about my signature Queen of Hearts effect—
the one that blew away everyone at his table. "That
will cost you something extra."

He arches an eyebrow in silent query.

"I want the video," I say. "Email it to me, and I'll
give you a hint."

Darian nods and swipes a few times on his phone.

"Done," he says. "Do you have it?"

I take out my own phone and wince. It's Sunday
night, right before the biggest opportunity of my life,
yet I have four messages from my boss.

Deciding to find out what the manipulative
bastard wants later, I go into my personal email and
verify that I have the video from Darian.

"Got it," I say. "Now about the Queen of Hearts
thing... If you're as observant and clever as I think you
are, you'll be able to guess my method tonight. Before
the main event, I'm going to perform that same effect
for Kacie."

"You sneaky minx." His green eyes fill with mirth.
"So you're not going to tell me?"

"A magician must always be at least one step
ahead of her audience." I give him the aloof smile
I've perfected over the years. "Do we have a deal or
not?"

"Fine. You win." He gracefully sits on the swivel
chair where I went through my eyebrow torture.
"Now, tell me, why did you look so spooked when I
first came in?"

I hesitate, then decide it will do no harm to admit

the truth. "It's because of that." I point at the screen where the live feed from the show is still rolling. At that precise moment, the camera pans to the large studio audience, all clapping at some nonsense the hostess said.

Darian looks amused. "Kacie? I didn't think that Muppet could frighten anyone."

"Not her." I wipe my damp palms on my leather jacket and learn that it's not the most absorbent of surfaces. "I'm afraid of speaking in front of people."

"You are? But you said you want to be a TV magician, and you perform at the restaurant all the time."

"The biggest audience at the restaurant is three or four people at a dinner table," I say. "In that studio over there, it's about a hundred. The fear kicks in after the numbers get into the teens."

Darian's amusement seems to deepen. "What about the millions of people who'll be watching you at home? Are you not worried about them?"

"I'm more worried about the studio audience, and yes, I understand the irony." I do my best not to get defensive. "For my own TV show, I'd do street magic with a small camera crew—that wouldn't trigger my fear too much."

Fear is actually an understatement. My attitude toward public speaking confirms the many studies showing that this particular phobia tends to be more pervasive than the fear of death. Certainly, I'd rather be eaten by a shark than have to appear in front of a big crowd.

After Darian called me about this opportunity, I learned how big the show's studio audience is, and I couldn't sleep for three days straight—which is why I feel like a Guantanamo Bay detainee on her way to enhanced interrogation. It's even worse than when I pulled a string of all-nighters for my stupid day job, and at the time, I thought it was the most stressful event of my life.

My roommate Ariel didn't give me her Valium lightly; it took a ton of persuasion on my part, and she only gave in when she could no longer bear to look at my miserable face.

Darian distracts me from my thoughts by fiddling with his phone again.

"This should inspire you," he says as soothing piano chords ring out of the tinny phone speaker. "It's a song about a man in a similar situation to yours."

It takes me a few moments to recognize the tune. Given that I last heard it when I was little, I up my estimate of Darian's age by an extra few years. The song is "Lose Yourself," from the *8 Mile* movie, where Eminem's character gets a chance to be a rapper. I guess my situation is similar enough, this being my big shot at what I want the most.

Unexpectedly, Darian begins to rap along with Eminem, and I fight an undignified giggle as some of the tension leaves my body. Do all British rappers sound as proper as the Queen?

"Now there's that smile," Darian says, unaware or uncaring that my grin is at his expense. "Keep it up."

He grabs the remote and turns up the volume on the TV in time for me to hear Kacie say, "Our hearts go out to the victims of the earthquake in Mexico. To donate to the Red Cross, please call the number at the bottom of the screen. And now, a quick commercial—"

"Sasha?" A man pops his head into the dressing room. "We need you on stage."

"Break a leg," Darian says and blows me an air kiss.

"In these shoes, I just might." I mime catching the kiss, throwing it on the floor, and stabbing it with my stiletto.

Darian's laugh grows distant as my guide and I leave the room, heading down a dark corridor. As we approach our destination, our steps seem to get louder, echoing in tune with my accelerating heartbeat. Finally, I see a light and hear the roar of the crowd.

This is how people going to face a firing squad must feel. If I weren't medicated, I'd probably bolt, my dreams be damned. As is, the guide has to grab my arm and drag me toward the light.

Apparently, the commercial break will soon be over.

"Go take a seat on the couch next to Kacie," someone whispers loudly into my ear. "And breathe."

My legs seem to grow heavier, each step a monumental effort of will. Hyperventilating, I step onto the platform where the couch is located and take tiny steps, trying to ignore the studio audience.

My dread is so extreme that time flows strangely; one moment I'm still walking, the next I'm standing by the couch.

I'm glad Kacie has her nose in a tablet. I'm not ready to exchange pleasantries when I have to do something as difficult as sitting down.

Knees shaking, I lower myself onto the couch like a fakir onto a bed of nails (which is not a feat of supernatural pain resistance, by the way, but the application of scientific principles of pressure).

Time distortion must've happened again, because the music signifying the commercial break comes to an abrupt close, and Kacie looks up from her tablet, her overly full lips stretching into a smile.

The pounding of my pulse is so loud in my ears I can't hear her greeting.

This is it.

I'm about to have a panic attack on national TV.

———

Order your copy of *The Girl Who Sees* today at www.dimazales.com!

About the Author

I love writing humor (often the inappropriate kind), happy endings (both kinds), and characters quirky enough to be called oddballs (because... balls). If you love your romance heavy on the comedy and feel-good vibes, visit mishabell.com and sign up for my newsletter.

Printed in Great Britain
by Amazon